BEHIND THE STONE HOUSE

DOROTHEA ANNA

Print: ISBN 9780578311746

E-book: ISBN 9780578311753

Printed in the United States of America

"A touching story about an endearing widow who risks everything to help a homeless man in desperate need."

— Michelle Godard-Richer, Writer

ACKNOWLEDGMENTS

Thanks always goes to God first, for the talent He gave me.

To my family's eternal support.

And to my awesome editor, D. A. Sarac and to my wonderful critique partners, Paul, Ellie, Trisha, Michelle, Scott, and the other Paul.

BEHIND THE STONE HOUSE

1
———

Gabrielle swallowed a sleeping pill and set the Dixie cup on the bathroom counter. In the mirror, green eyes drained of life stared back at her.

She sighed and turned off the light, pausing in the stillness of the dark surrounding her, wondering if this was what one faced when leaving this life for the next.

Pushing aside those thoughts that often swirled in her head, Gabrielle kept to her nightly ritual by descending the stairs to the dimly lit living room.

She approached the vigil lamp hanging from the wooden icon shelf on the wall. The flame's tip peeked over the edge of the kandelia. She added olive oil to the glass holder, and the floating wick rose like a flag on a pole, adding a yellow glow to the shadowed living space.

A silver-framed picture of Andrew sat below the shelf. In the soft, hazy light from the oil lamp, Andrew's fathomless blue eyes gazed at her. His usual amiable smile brightened his face, and his sandy-blond hair cut short with loose bangs brushed across his eyebrows. A small glass vase with a handful of white roses stood in front of the photo.

With shaky fingers, Gabrielle touched his face.

Andrew had left this earth forever.

She closed her eyes in silent prayer and waited for the blanket of solace to surround her. For those few quiet moments, the ache in her heart and the emptiness inside her receded.

Soon the drowsiness of Ambien would pull her into a dreamless slumber—the only way she got any sleep these past few months.

A storm outside rattled the picture window's panes. She pulled back the transparent yellow curtain, and a flash of lightning lit up the sky. The wind groaned, sweeping raindrops across the glass pane facing the backyard. Two oaks flanked a bench with two decaying jack-o'-lanterns sitting on it, transforming them into a blackened blur like midnight-blue oil smeared across a canvas.

The house squeaked in protest against the gusts battering its sides, and a chill crept into the living room.

If Andrew were still with her, they'd be snuggling on the couch, watching a movie or roasting marshmallows. She frowned, moved to the fireplace, and stacked three logs packaged in paper into its ashy stomach. Grabbing some kindling and a match, she placed the wood chips on the logs, lit the match, touched it to the kindling and paper, igniting them, then tossed the stick onto the timber pile. As the flames grew, she went to the sofa and curled her legs under her.

Through the picture window, another spark of light tore through the evening's firmament, illuminating the trees and bench. A movement caught her eye. A shadowy shape—a blur before her—darted from behind the oaks, then disappeared into the darkness as a crack of thunder boomed.

Amid the climbing drowsiness of her medication, Gabrielle pressed a hand to her chest. She went to the front door and checked the lock. It was secured.

She inspected the kitchen door as well. It, too, was locked. She peeked out the kitchen window where one of the trees and her small bed of hearty petunias swayed in the wind.

Perhaps she'd imagined it. The eyes played tricks on a person in the dark. And her mind was a mess. Gabrielle had been walking through life in a numbing haze for six months.

She glanced toward the window again and clasped together her trembling hands. She didn't have Andrew to protect her from danger if there was anything nefarious out there.

Gabrielle shuffled to the couch, picked up the soft afghan resting on top of it, and sat down. She shook the blanket open and covered her body. The fire crackled with warmth and light.

She shifted her gaze once more toward the window and the night sky. Why had she been so afraid? If anything had been in her yard, it had probably been an animal. After all, she lived in a rural area where many different animals wandered her property. And when had she started to care about her life again? Or was the whole reaction just instinctive? No thought process to it whatsoever. She shook her head, her mind soupy.

Gabrielle closed her eyes and ran a hand over the gold band on her ring finger. All that mattered in her life had died with Andrew. How had she managed to get out of bed for the past six months? She laid a wrist on her forehead. She'd had no other choice. But all those months had meant nothing to her. Would that ever change?

GABRIELLE'S ALARM SHRILLED, pulling her out of a groggy, drug-induced sleep. She splashed her face several times with water from the bathroom sink, its coolness slicing through the last effects of her medicated state.

She stumbled into the kitchen to fill the teakettle with

water. Out the window, the sun's crown burst from the horizon, a brilliant soft pink and a tint of blazing orange. Last night's storm had toppled one of the jack-o'-lanterns from its perch on the metal bench where it now lay on the brown grass, its impish face toward the ground—gifts from her niece and nephew for Halloween, which had come and gone two weeks ago with little fanfare for Gabrielle. The pumpkins' deformed shapes and rotting insides told her it was time to toss them. She made a mental note to do so after work.

The seasons changed too quickly, and Thanksgiving was approaching. Gabrielle frowned. This year she'd be hard-pressed to find something to be thankful for. Her heart wasn't in it. And she definitely wasn't ready to face Christmas—the first Christmas without Andrew. The thought of decorating a tree and attending Nativity services without her husband left her hollow inside.

The teapot whistled. Gabrielle turned off the stove, then poured the hot water into a mug with a peppermint tea bag in it —her drink every morning for as long as she could remember. It had become such a routine, such a habit she couldn't function very well without it.

After steeping the bag in hot liquid, she sat at the kitchen table and took a sip. Just breathing in the peppermint boosted her mood.

Before Andrew's death, she'd meet weekly with her best friend Karensa over tea. The couple of times when Karensa had attempted to persuade her to continue their get-togethers, part of Gabrielle listened, and the other part settled in her usual fog of feeling nothing and feeling everything. Maybe she'd make the effort this week to set up a time to meet with her friend. The thought fizzled as she contemplated having to make small talk and pretend to enjoy the visit.

Gabrielle set down her empty cup, sighed, and plodded out of the kitchen.

ON HER WAY to the architectural firm where she worked, the morning of the accident surfaced in her mind.

"Have a good day, and don't worry about printing out the theater tickets. I'll do that before I leave the house. Love you!" The words floated through her mind. They were the last words she'd spoken to Andrew before he'd driven off to work.

An hour later, a police officer stood on their front porch with a grimace on his face. He'd explained what had happened to Andrew—the near head-on with a truck, before careening into the stocky elm—

No. She wouldn't relive the terrible crash again. How many times would she repeat this in her brain before the vivid details would cease to haunt her? She bit her quivering lip, punched the button on the radio in the car, and turned up the volume. Sinatra crooned about love being a tender trap, and she let his soothing voice drown out her inner thoughts.

Gabrielle parked in her usual spot three spaces from the building's glass front doors and climbed out of the car. The morning air bit into her exposed face as she did her regular scanning of the parking lot—a basic instinct for a woman alone in the city. Next to the large green dumpster on the left side of her office edifice sat a man with disheveled dark blond hair, wearing a gray jacket, faded jeans, and well-worn sneakers. A frayed black backpack lay next to him.

She sucked in her breath. *Andrew?*

The man's head was down, his knees bent, his arms rested on top of them, hands loosely clasped. He looked up at her. Even though he must have been twenty feet from her, his startling blue eyes shone intensely above an unkempt beard. Those eyes. Andrew's eyes. Gabrielle moved with a sense of desperation toward the man. When she was no more than three feet away, she stopped. What was he doing here?

"Jordan?" Her foggy breath floated in the crisp air.

He got up from the ground. "Gabby."

"What are you doing here? What happened to you?"

Andrew's cousin shrugged. "I've got nowhere else to go."

"What do you mean? Are you—?"

"Homeless?" He eyed her as if expecting her to cringe with disdain.

"I didn't mean—"

"Yes."

She moved closer to him. "What happened?"

"Lost my job six months ago. Company closed, got laid off. Couldn't pay rent, the bills. My roommate didn't like that and kicked me out. Been four months now."

Six months ago. Around the time of Andrew's death. She swallowed hard as the pain from that time rolled through her. It seemed like only a few weeks ago that he'd left her. She wiped her sniffly nose, her mind overwhelmed with images of Andrew.

"—never can tell who's a true friend."

She pushed the thoughts from her mind and focused on Jordan, who resembled Andrew so much it hurt her heart and made it swell all at once. "Oh right. Not a real friend." She glanced back at her office building. "But why were you sitting in this lot?"

"I remember Andrew telling me you worked here. You're my last chance."

"Last chance?"

"Yeah. Been trying to get a job, but there don't seem to be any. I used to be an architect. Thought maybe you could find out if your company is hiring." He patted his ratty jacket. "Can't go in looking like this."

He wanted her to help him. She rubbed her temple. Did she have the energy or will to do that?

"Hey, if it's too much to ask, just say so." He looked toward the street, his face pinched.

Guilt nudged her. Jordan was Andrew's cousin, a part of him. She needed to make an effort. Andrew would want her to. "No, it's not too much. I can ask Tom, our HR guy. But what if he doesn't have any openings? I'm just the receptionist there, but the second floor is full of architects."

He shrugged. "Got no other choice but to keep looking."

Where had he been sleeping while living on the streets? "It'll be winter soon." The frigid air encompassed them. "Scratch that. It's already here even if the calendar says otherwise."

"Yeah, I know."

"Well, you can't stay out here during the winter months."

Jordan scratched the side of his bearded face. "What do you expect me to do?"

She racked her brain for ideas. "I—"

Two cars drove into the parking lot and slid into the spaces next to hers.

She checked her watch. "Listen, I've got to get inside." She glanced at the people emerging from their vehicles as they took one look at her, said something to each other, and headed into the building. She could imagine what they were saying... *Who is that scruffy guy with Gabby?*

"Hey, you've got a job to do. Don't worry about me. I know my way around these streets." Jordan shoved his hands into his worn jeans pockets.

She pursed her lips. He wasn't making her situation easy. She glanced from Jordan to the office and back at him. "Will you be here around five this evening?"

"I can be," he said.

"Good. I'll hopefully have an answer for you then."

"'Kay."

She studied his frame. "Have you had any breakfast? How do you eat?"

"There's a soup kitchen a couple of streets over. Food's served every afternoon."

"But that's not breakfast."

"I eat when I can."

She pictured the spread of coffee and donuts that greeted her at her office each day. "Hold on. I'll bring you something to eat."

Gabrielle hurried to the front doors of the office, used her key fob to unlock the door, and ran in. Just as she thought, the donut boxes were open and spread out on the break table in the small kitchen. The aroma of coffee drifted in the warm air. She selected a chocolate and a glazed donut, picked up a napkin, filled a Styrofoam cup with coffee, and rushed out the door.

She approached Jordan and handed him the coffee and donuts. He stared at them as if he'd never seen donuts before.

"They're not the healthiest food, but it's something."

His gaze rose from the food to her eyes. A grin broke through his whiskered face. "Thanks."

That smile was so much like Andrew's. Beautiful, authentic. "You're welcome." She rubbed her hands together to brush off crumbs. "Remember to be here at five."

"Yeah, I'll remember." Jordan sipped the coffee.

"Good." She managed a half smile as Jordan walked away.

She'd accomplished the obligation to her husband in helping his cousin, despite it draining the little energy she had. Come five o'clock, maybe she'd have some good news for Jordan.

2

———

By midafternoon, the niggling duty to reach out to Tom, the HR director, loomed over Gabrielle like a work-related deadline. The stress of having to do this invaded her comfortable, numb state and caused her stomach to churn. But she needed to remember that this was for Andrew. Jordan was his cousin.

She met with Tom at four thirty, and just as she'd suspected, there were no current openings. She shrugged and rolled her head to release the tension. Well, she'd tried.

Jordan's downtrodden expression when he'd been sitting by the dumpster came back to her. She wasn't looking forward to passing along the bad news.

When five o'clock arrived, she bundled up and walked toward the lot. But Jordan wasn't there.

The wind had picked up, blowing ice-cold air against her body. Despite the red knit scarf hugging her neck, she scrunched her shoulders. The air smelled like winter.

The sun hovered over the horizon in between the city's towering buildings. It was that time of year when the light of the day was lost. A fitting season for her somber mood.

Gabrielle checked her watch again. Five minutes after five. She blew out a puffy white sigh. Where could he be? She clasped her hands together. Maybe he wasn't coming, and she could hold off telling him the bad news until tomorrow, or whenever he decided to return. *If* he returned. The burden weighing heavily on her shoulders lifted at the thought. She could go home now, worry-free.

She peered at the dumpster again. Jordan stood there. She blinked, wondering if it was an apparition. He folded his arms against the merciless, frigid breeze.

"Jordan." She walked over to him, keeping her head down to protect her face.

"Sorry. Don't have a watch. Had to ask the time from an old man down the street."

No watch? The thought hadn't crossed her mind. Did he still have a cell phone, or was that gone too? She frowned. Everyone in her world had a job and a house or apartment to live in. She'd been blessed with a place to live. Yet at one time so had Jordan.

"It's okay. I'm sorry. I hadn't thought about you not having a watch."

"I had one, but I hocked it to buy some food last month."

His reality sank in, and everything about his situation came into sharp focus.

Against the icy wind, he stomped his feet and patted his arms. "Did you talk to somebody?"

She tensed, even though she knew the question was going to come up. She hesitated, studying his shaking figure.

He glanced up from tucking his face in the top of his jacket. "Guess not."

"No, I did." She looked away and rubbed her gloved hands together, giving herself a moment before answering. "I talked to Tom."

"Yeah?"

She shook her head with lips folded in. "I'm sorry. There aren't any openings right now."

"Figured. But thanks for asking." He blew out a breath, then pivoted toward the street.

Relieved he'd received the bad news all right, she caught hold of his arm. The need to make it up to him in another way nagged her. The gloomy gray surroundings swept by the icy breeze gave her an idea of how to fix the situation, even though the thought made her squirm with discomfort. "Where are you going to sleep tonight?"

"Probably the usual spot."

"Where's that?"

"Some old cardboard boxes in an alley a few streets down from here."

"Cardboard boxes?" She imagined him curled up in a box that swayed from the night's gusts.

"Yeah. They keep me pretty warm when the shelters are full." He coughed. "Just have to watch for the critters that want to join me."

Her body tensed. "Critters?"

"You know. Rats, raccoons, 'possums." He bent his head, and the top of his jacket covered his mouth.

She hugged herself. "Jordan, you shouldn't stay out here tonight. It's too cold—"

"Don't worry about me. I'll be fine." He scowled. "I can take care of myself."

"I'm sure, but—"

"Yeah, I know. You feel sorry for me. I get it."

"Don't put words in my mouth," Gabrielle grumbled, not appreciating his snotty attitude. She had enough to deal with. "I don't feel sorry for you."

His brows lifted.

"I was a little concerned. And I never said you couldn't take care of yourself."

She pushed aside the stupid thoughts of doing anything for him. But when his eyes and mouth drooped in a pitiful display of remorse, her walls fell, and the plan resurfaced.

"I have an extra bedroom at my house that you're welcome to use. You'll be out of the cold for the night."

He shook his head as another blast of icy air fanned their exposed faces. "Thanks, but I'm not going to burden you. I'll be fine."

Her muscles relaxed. His answer made it easy for her, took away the stress and left the ball in his court, and hopefully it would stay there. She'd made the effort that Andrew would've wanted her to. Her conscience was clear.

"Andrew and me... we were close," he said. "You've gone through enough."

Yes, she had. Tears stung her eyes at the sound of Andrew's name. She'd cried so much already. Yet the tears always returned. Would she ever be able to function without swollen eyelids and a stuffy nose? Did she really want to? She shook her head, working to sweep out the cluttered emotions swimming around in her mind.

Jordan grabbed his backpack and walked away.

Her heart sank. She glanced skyward. *Did I mess up, love? Should I have convinced him to go to our home?* What a mess. Her mind was muddled, as usual.

Gabrielle watched him amble down the sidewalk. If anything happened to him, would she be to blame? How would Andrew feel about her leaving his cousin out on the streets, especially since she seemed to be Jordan's last hope?

She pressed her lips together. But Jordan wanted it this way. She couldn't control him and didn't want to.

Gabrielle headed to her car, got in, and slammed the door

shut. She started the vehicle and let it warm up, then turned on the radio to clear her mind. Ella Fitzgerald's soulful voice caressed the air as she rubbed her gloved hands together to generate warmth.

At home, Gabrielle started a fire in the hearth. She slipped off her black pumps as images of Jordan sleeping in those boxes in a dark alley harassed her thoughts. She huffed. It was his choice, and she needed to remember that.

The cozy living room held a beige sofa, a maroon-and-forest-green glider, and an inherited mahogany coffee table from her parents. Her favorite wooden lamp featuring a carved bear clinging to its cylindrical base sat on the oak end table. She'd picked that up when she and Andrew had vacationed in Estes Park, Colorado, three years ago for their fifth wedding anniversary. They could never have enough decorative bears in their home. Now she'd have to add to their collection on her own.

Before sorrow had a chance to overtake her, the house phone rang. Her mother's number glowed on the landline's screen, and she answered.

"Gabrielle, honey, how was work?" Her mother's soft voice came through the earpiece.

"Hey, Mom." She sank onto the couch. "Same as it always is."

"How are you feeling? Are you keeping warm?"

"I'm feeling all right." Not really, but she wouldn't worry her mother any more than she already did.

"I hope you're not keeping things to yourself for my benefit."

Sighing quietly, she said, "I'm doing as well as can be expected. How are you?"

"Well, that's an improvement from the last time we talked."

"How are you doing?"

"Why are we talking about me? I'm perfectly fine. Tell me, are you going to come over for Thanksgiving next Thursday?"

Next Thursday? Thanksgiving? Already?

"Gabrielle?"

"Yes, sorry. I hadn't realized Thanksgiving was so soon."

"Ah," her mother said and followed it with a tsk. "Time flies by."

"It not only flies by, it's left me behind..."

"Sweetheart, I know this time of year is so hard. But your sister and her family will be in town. We'd all love to see you."

She and Andrew had wanted to start a family, but after trying for four years, they'd resigned to the fact they weren't going to be able to have any children... at least not through natural means. They'd discussed adopting, but all the red tape, paperwork, and cost halted that endeavor.

Envy stung Gabrielle as she thought about her sister's perfect family. Her husband of fifteen years, their successful restaurant in Columbus, Ohio, and their son and daughter, both in grade school, four years apart, with top marks in academics and busy playing musical instruments, sports, and taking dance. All of which Andrew and she had longed for but could never attain. Andrew had worked hard, teaching young teens world history, and she'd worked just as diligently at the architectural firm. They'd learned to live a modest life and accepted whatever —good or bad— that came upon them.

"Gabrielle, are you listening to me?"

"Yes, Mom. I'll be there."

"Wonderful."

"What time should I come?"

"Noon would be great."

"Okay."

Their conversation ended, and she went to the kitchen to heat up leftover lentil soup.

Less than an hour later, a knock sounded at her door. Who could that be? She wasn't expecting anyone.

She opened the door and found her best friend trembling on the porch. Her curly black hair bounced in the wind. "Rensa."

Karensa rubbed her gloved hands together. "Ohhh, it's freezing and it's not even winter yet." She bobbed her head side to side, looking past Gabrielle's shoulders. "Are you going to let me in or leave me to freeze to death out here?"

Gabrielle stepped aside for her friend to enter.

"It's too cold for November." Karensa bent down and pulled off her shoes.

They went into the living room where she removed her coat, scarf, and gloves and set them on the sofa. Karensa headed to the hearth and warmed her hands in front of the orange flames licking the three logs.

"We didn't have plans for tonight. I'm not—"

"It's time you did." Karensa gave Gabrielle a chiding stare as if she were her mother. "I haven't seen you in a month, Gabby."

Gabrielle looked away and focused on the picture of Andrew at the prayer shelf. "I haven't felt up to getting together."

Her friend put an arm around her and gave her a gentle squeeze. "I know, love, but it's good to spend time with your best friend. I'm here for you. I *want* to be here for you."

She studied Karensa. Did she have it in her to be engaging? She sighed. Well, her friend was there, and she'd have to make the best of it.

Gabrielle went into the kitchen and filled the teapot and set it on the burner. Setting two mugs on the counter next to the stove, she listened to Karensa vent about her unruly coworkers. A crisis at her friend's workplace popped up more often than a teenager's pimples.

She dropped a peppermint bag in one mug and chamomile in the other.

Karensa appeared in the doorway to the kitchen. "Anyway, how was your day?"

She poured hot water into the mugs, then set them on the table. "The usual. Same old routine every day."

"Yeah, I know how that is." Karensa inspected her from her seat. "Have the nightmares of the accident stopped?"

"No." She sat and gripped her cup. This was why she didn't want to meet with Karensa or anyone. The constant questions about how she was, the accident, missing Andrew, the looks of pity. She couldn't bear it. But she swallowed hard and tried to remember her friend meant well, and she'd be honest as she always was. "The accident report came back to me this morning."

Karensa glanced down at her drink. "I'm sorry, love."

She shrugged, then took a sip of her tea. "It's just the way it is."

Karensa didn't reply.

She glanced at her. "I did manage to stop before the whole tragedy ran through my head."

"That's progress."

"I suppose."

"I know I've brought this up before, but it was early on, and you weren't thinking clearly then... Have you thought about talking with a counselor? Maybe a support group?"

Gabrielle fidgeted in her chair. "It crossed my mind." But she had no desire to talk about her husband's death and their life with anyone, let alone a therapist. "I've been in touch with Father Christopher. That's all I need right now." Okay. So she hadn't spoken to her spiritual father since a month after Andrew's death when he called to check on her, but it wasn't a lie. They had been in touch.

"That's good. At least you're talking to someone. But please leave a door open for a professional. A therapist can help you get through your grief." Karensa raised her mug to her lips, her brown eyes on Gabrielle.

She winced. Too often in the past month, Karensa and her mother had tried to encourage her to work through her grief and live the life she had, but their well-meant words always sliced through her, adding resentment to her hurt. He'd died just six months ago, and she had a right to grieve as long as she needed. Besides, she'd miss him forever. How could she not?

"Don't think I'm expecting you to get over Andrew in a matter of months. It's silly to even think that."

It was as if her friend had read her mind.

Karensa set down her cup. "I just want you to be able to get to the point where you're focused on the good memories of your life together." She leaned her elbow on the table and rested her chin on her hand. "Does that make sense?"

Gabrielle swallowed the lump in her throat and smiled. "It does. Thanks."

"Of course, love."

She took another sip of tea.

"So, I guess we both had boring workdays. Nothing to really blab about." Karensa snickered.

Jordan came to mind. "Actually, something out of the ordinary *did* happen."

"Really? Like what?" Karensa's eyes widened, and she straightened in her chair.

"I saw Andrew's cousin, Jordan, this morning."

"Jordan?" Karensa's forehead furrowed. "It's been a while since I've heard that name."

"I hadn't seen him since last Christmas at Andrew's parents' house."

"That's kind of nice, isn't it, that you were able to run into him?"

"The circumstances didn't make it exactly a cheerful reunion."

Karensa frowned. "What happened?"

"He's living on the street, Rensa."

She gaped. "He's homeless?"

"Yes."

"Lord, have mercy. How'd he end up homeless?"

She told Karensa everything about her encounter with Jordan and offering her extra bedroom to him.

"That was more than generous of you."

"Yes, but he refused."

Karensa patted Gabrielle's hand, then held her mug. "You did all you could. You can't help someone who doesn't want to be helped."

She nodded, the worry and tension leaving her with her friend's logical and affirming support. "Thanks for confirming what I'd been thinking since I drove home from work."

"Good. Glad I could help clear up any confusion."

Doubt slid through Gabrielle's stomach. She couldn't completely disregard her thoughts on how Andrew would feel about this situation with Jordan. It was as if she could feel Andrew's finger poking against her ribs in some mystical way, urging her to help his cousin even though Jordan had no interest in being helped. That was the real conundrum. She grimaced.

Karensa stared at her with the look of someone who knew her too well. "Uh-oh. What happened? Your half smile turned to a frown in seconds."

"There's another element to this problem."

"What's that?"

"Andrew."

Karensa's brows came together. "What does he have to do with this?"

"Jordan is Andrew's cousin."

"Yeah. I know, love. What are you getting at?"

"I owe it to Andrew to help his cousin in any way I can."

Karensa shook her head. "But you just said he doesn't want your help."

"Well—"

Karensa tilted her chin up. "What about his own family? Can't they help him out?"

"I don't know. I'd have to find out."

"How old is Jordan now?"

Andrew, a year older than her, had been thirty-two when he'd died. Jordan was a few years younger. "He's twenty-eight."

"So, he's pushing thirty, well into adulthood." Karensa took a sip of her tea.

"Yes, I know, but—"

"But what, Gabby? What do you think you can do for the grown man who's chosen to live on the streets rather than get a job?"

She couldn't believe her big-hearted friend. How could she think Jordan hadn't tried for a job? "Come on, Rensa. He's been trying to get a job since he lost the one six months ago. The problem is nobody will give him a chance."

Karensa tapped her chin for a moment before responding. "I admit that jobs are hard to come by these days."

"Yes."

"But that still doesn't change the fact that he doesn't want your help."

"Let's give it a little bit of time." Did she really think Jordan would change his mind in the coming days? It didn't matter. The expansive light of desire to help began to burn away the gray cobwebs of despondency in her soupy mind.

Karensa pushed back her chair and stood up, giving Gabrielle a doubtful look. "Give it some time? You think he's going to change his mind?"

She glanced out the window. A breeze fluttered through the few leaves left on the trees. "Winter is coming."

"So, you think he'll bend because of snow?"

"When it's below freezing... Don't you think?"

"I don't—"

"But I can't wait until then." She rose from her chair, gripped her mug, and followed Karensa into the living room.

They sat on the couch. "How do you plan to get him to change his mind? And do you really think it's a good idea?"

The mysterious niggling in her ribs and picking at her brain to help Jordan grew more persistent. "I feel compelled to do this. Andrew would want me to help his cousin." She turned her cup in slow circles on her thigh. "He's giving me signs that I need to help Jordan."

Karensa raised her hands in the air and let them flop into her lap. "Oh well, I can't win against that." She tilted her head to the side, her expression thoughtful. "You've got the spiritual world behind you. And even if you didn't, you're too stubborn for me or anyone else to ever change your mind."

Gabrielle couldn't help but laugh. She couldn't argue with her friend about her stubbornness. It was as though she were born with it, and the trait would make itself known throughout the years, whether peddling off on her bike through a rainstorm to the local store to get her favorite chocolate bars her mother was out of or driving off to Pittsburgh for a signed Pirates T-shirt for Andrew that no local or online store carried. It was the perfect Christmas gift for him and had been worth the eight-hour trip.

"So, what's your plan?"

"Well, I'm hoping to talk him into staying at my house at least a few nights a week when the shelters are closed. And I want to help him find a job." Just thinking about it drained Gabrielle of energy, but this wasn't about her; it was about Andrew. She'd work to focus on him and his cousin.

Karensa raised her brows. "I hope he gives in."

"So do I." The sooner she got this problem solved, the better.

When Karensa left, Gabrielle filled the oil lamp, then climbed the stairs to her bedroom.

Entering the room, she glanced at the stack of historical books from the Civil War up to the Vietnam War on Andrew's nightstand. They still lay there, never to be read by her love. Beside the books sat a picture of her and Andrew beaming with arms around each other at a friend's birthday party two years ago. A flood of bittersweet memories filled her. She laid a hand on her chest as she worked to stave the emotions swirling inside her.

Gabrielle opened the two-door closet across from their bed and pushed back the doors in search of Andrew's sleepwear. She'd been wearing his green cotton top to bed since his death. Now that it was colder, she wanted one of his warmer tops to snuggle in with her own pink pajama bottoms.

His clothes lay on various plastic-coated wire shelves in the middle of the rectangular space. As she pulled out his pajama top, a folded piece of paper emerged from amid the stack underneath his pajamas and fell on the wood floor. She picked it up and opened the paper, which had another sheet folded inside of it. They were small pieces like the type one uses to jot down numbers next to the home phone. Why hadn't she seen those before? She read the inside note first:

Hey, Andy,

Are you making progress on the surprise? I know you've been at it for two months now. She's going to be stoked! Let me know if I can help in any way. —J

Surprise? What surprise had Andrew been planning? Were they talking about her? And was the person with the initial *J* possibly Jordan? She slid this sheet behind the other one and immediately recognized Andrew's slanted cursive writing scrawled across the page:

Hey, J,

I haven't gotten it all together yet, and I don't want to tell her until I have the final piece. Yes, she'll be so excited, but she'll know at the right time when I, alone, can tell her. —Andy

The fact that Andrew had still written notes nearly had her in nostalgic giggles. The last time Andrew wrote any letters, they were to her during their dating years. He'd stuff little love notes in her purse without her knowledge. Once they'd married, he'd leave notes on her pillow in the mornings when he'd be up and out the door before she'd woken. Andrew preferred writing things, especially since he worked with physical pencils and papers in his classroom, over utilizing his cell phone's text capabilities. He was her favorite romantic retro nerd.

Coming back to the present, she tried to process the notes. Since she hadn't had it in her to move any of his things since his death, she wondered what else she'd find in the subsequent weeks when she mustered up the courage to sort through his belongings.

Gabrielle read the notes again. Why wasn't this note given to whoever *J* was? If *J* was Jordan, could he hold the answers? Or was the mystery gift gone with Andrew?

3

F rost glistened on the patch of grass across from Gabrielle's office. Overnight, the temperature had dipped below freezing, but thankfully, the wind had abated and she didn't have to bear it this morning.

But Jordan did.

Did he make it through the night in those flimsy cardboard boxes? Where was he now?

She entered her office building, the questions lingering.

Gabrielle managed to stay busy and make the deadlines for the day, keeping thoughts of Jordan at bay.

After work, she crossed the few feet of asphalt toward the building's dumpster where Jordan lay curled and shaking on the ground.

"Oh my god. Jordan." Gabrielle squatted and touched his shoulder.

He mumbled something incoherent. Looking up at her, his face had taken on a reddish hue and glistened with sweat, leaving sections of his tousled, oily hair wet.

She squeezed his shoulder. "Are you sick?"

He let out a violent seal cough, sniffled, and wiped his nose with the back of his hand. "Yeah."

"Come on." She pulled gently on his arm and tried to help him stand.

"I'm okay. Let go." He broke free from her grip and fell to his knees on the hard cement.

"No, you're not okay, and you're coming with me." Gabrielle grabbed his backpack, then pulled on his arm as he stood up.

She led him to her car and opened the passenger-side door. Grunting, he climbed in and collapsed against the seat. She tossed his pack in the back seat, shut the door, and hurried around to the driver's side.

"Put on your seat belt." She turned the key in the ignition, and the car rumbled to life.

She'd never been a fan of macho men. Thankfully, it had been one of the few traits Andrew hadn't shared with Jordan. She drove out of the lot and onto the road for home.

———

GABRIELLE PARKED in the one-car detached garage to the left of her house, got out, and helped Jordan to his feet. They walked slowly through the cold evening air to the front door. Inside, she took off her gloves and coat while Jordan coughed and shivered beside her.

In the darkened room, she switched on the bear lamp, then guided Jordan to the couch. She crossed to the hearth and lit a fire. It slowly grew, giving off welcomed heat and light.

As Jordan lay back on the sofa, Gabrielle grabbed the afghan blanket atop the glider. She spread it over Jordan's quaking body.

"I'll find some Advil and make chamomile tea."

After taking the ibuprofen and drinking the tea, Jordan

leaned his head against the fat arm of the couch and stared at the glowing flames in the hearth.

"Did you sleep all night in the alley?" she asked.

His weary stare traveled to her. "Yeah."

She shook her head. Why hadn't he listened to her? "See? Last night was too cold to be out there in whatever boxes you managed to scrounge up."

He hacked out a rattling cough. "I was already feeling like crap before last night." His eyes left hers and gazed, once again, at the burning embers.

"It's been freezing the past three days, and without a good, warm place—"

"Yeah, I know." Jordan gave her a narrowed sideways glance and sniffled. "Quit talking to me like I'm stupid."

His grumpiness had returned. Why did she bother bringing him home? *For Andrew. You keep forgetting this.* She sighed and glanced at the ceiling. *How am I doing?* She winced, then grabbed a box of tissue from the bathroom and handed him one. "You're not stupid, just stubborn."

He took a tissue and wiped his nose.

She sat down on the glider kitty-corner to the couch and studied him. "Why hasn't your family helped you? Where are they?"

"They're in Pittsburg. Not exactly close."

"Yes, but you're their son. Why didn't they come for you months ago and take you home with them?"

"Mom's dead, and Pop doesn't give a damn about me." He scowled.

She frowned. "I'm sorry."

"There's nothing to be sorry about. I'm not." His features hardened in the firelight.

She didn't know what to say, so she said nothing. She gazed at the indigo sky through the window. Cloudless, the firmament held several dazzling stars and a luminous three-quarter moon. How could the world outside look so beautiful, so calm in the midst of a house without Andrew and with his cousin lying across from her, burning with fever?

When she turned back to Jordan, his eyes were closed, his mouth open, letting out gentle, rumbling snores. She pulled the blanket over his shoulders.

Switching off the bear lamp, Gabrielle headed to the kandelia and added oil to the glass cup. She went to the kitchen sink, filled a small watering can, and returned to the prayer mantelpiece and table. She added water to the vase with the roses. Setting down the can, Gabrielle gazed at the picture of Andrew. "Honey, I need your help with Jordan." She pressed her index and middle fingers against her lips, then placed them on his smiling face.

THE NEXT MORNING, Gabrielle came downstairs to make tea. Jordan wasn't on the couch, in the living room, anywhere. He must have left while she'd been in her deep, medicated sleep. Judging by his condition last night, she didn't think he would get very far on foot.

Bundled up, she walked to the garage. She scanned her property for Jordan. He wasn't there.

Worry gnawed at her. Had he passed out somewhere in the woods situated a hundred feet behind her house? The urge to check had her black boots stamping the hard, frosty ground in the direction of the forest. The morning's pink sun peeked over the horizon, sending shafts of rosy light through the trees. White puffs of air flowed from her mouth as she trod ahead, crunching on pine needles and leaves littering the ground.

The dense part of the woods ahead of her closed off the rays from the sun and gave her a feeling of dread. Hearing only the sound of the dried leaves crackling under her boots, she stopped and surveyed the area. Her breathing pulsed in the mossy, damp air. Her heart thumped in her ears.

Something told her to get out of there.

Just as she pivoted toward the way she'd come, leaves rustled, and tree branches snapped to her right. She looked where the sound came from and saw the flicker of a human figure in the gray mass of trees.

"Jor—?" The word caught in her throat.

Ten feet away, a stocky, grungy man paused between two trees. He wore shoddy clothes and a tattered blue bandanna around his head. His cold eyes glared back at her, and his lip curled in a menacing snarl. Hands fisted at his side.

Chills crept down her spine before panic hit her. She ran toward the opening in the forest, crunching and scattering leaves in her wake.

Gabrielle reached the garage before she looked back, huffing and bending over, out of breath. A shaky sigh escaped from her mouth as she scanned the area for the creepy man. He didn't appear. She scrambled to her car, got in, and drove down the path toward the main road, relieved to be away from her own property.

On the short ride to work, she gripped the steering wheel as apprehension settled in her chest. Where would this man be when she came home tonight? Worry haunted her throughout the day, distracting her from focusing on her work.

Without any solution coming to mind, Gabrielle would have to face this uncertainty alone in the coming hours.

4

After work, Gabrielle drove at a snail's pace around town, passing by the homeless shelter several times. No sign of Jordan. At this point, what mattered was she wasn't home alone. She'd managed to wander around, safe in her car on the streets of Lancaster for over an hour.

Her car rolled down the gravel road and into her garage by six thirty. Karensa would be there at seven. For once, she was glad she'd given in to Karensa's insistence that they meet again so soon. She pried her sore hands from the steering wheel.

The sun had set, and only a glimmer of yellow-white light on the horizon remained. She turned off the engine, leaving the lights shining on the wooden wall of the old building where bush pruners, gardening gloves, and other tools hung on pegs. The silence surrounding her should have been a comfort, but instead, it intensified her anxiousness. Was he out there waiting to jump her before she could reach the back door? Her muscles tightened. She lived on an isolated property where the closest neighbor was half a mile away.

The heat leftover in the car had evaporated, and the chill of the outside air crept into the vehicle. She switched off the lights and took a deep breath, steadying herself as she climbed out of the car.

Gabrielle walked stiffly in the frosty air toward her old stone house. The scent of a smoking chimney drifted in the light breeze—usually a comforting smell for her, but tension and fear snaking through her didn't allow it.

The large elms, metal bench, and rotting pumpkins came into view as she crossed a small swath of the yard toward the back door. The note to herself about throwing out the jack-o'-lanterns came back to her. She veered her path toward them.

As she picked up both of them, the flitting figure she thought she'd seen the other night surfaced in her mind. She froze and scanned the browning backyard, the hill beyond the garage, and the ebony forest straight ahead in the distance. Her breathing punctuated the dead quiet around her.

The evening sky blotted out the last of the setting sun's light as she quickened her pace back to the left side of the garage where the trash totes sat. Lifting the lid, she threw the pumpkins into the container where they landed with two hollow clunks, then jogged over to the back door. She dug in her coat pocket for the keys, opened the door, and slammed it behind her.

Relieved to be inside her home, she glanced at the clock on the kitchen wall that read six forty-five. Fifteen more minutes until Karensa would be there. Gabrielle let out a ragged sigh of relief and locked the back door. She removed her boots, then crossed the white tile to the living room, peeling off her gloves, coat, and scarf and hanging them on the wooden peg shelf by the front door.

The moon peeked through the large window behind the couch as the faint lingering scent of a burned-out wick floated through the warm room. Before tending to the oil, she turned on the bear lamp to illuminate the plastic container of beeswax wicks on the table below the kandelia. She stuck a fresh wick in the cork, filled the glass in the lamp, placed the cork in the oil-filled cup, and lit the wick. The icon of archangel Gabriel gazed at her with his face and halo glistening from the glow of the little orange flame. Crossing herself, she said a prayer for Jordan and for Andrew's soul, then headed to the kitchen to start dinner.

GABRIELLE OPENED the front door for her friend.

Karensa flashed a smile as she pulled off her red mittens. "Hey."

"Hey."

Karensa removed her brown suede boots and padded her way to the living room. She stopped, looked at the hearth, then Gabrielle. "What? No fire?"

"Sorry. My routine was disrupted this evening." She glanced at the blackness outside the window by the front door. After encountering the man in the woods, she became more and more convinced the figure in her backyard had been real.

"Disrupted? What happened?" Karensa sat on the couch, leaning forward with her elbows on her knees.

Gabrielle sat next to her. "This morning I saw a man in the woods behind the house."

"What? What did he do?"

"Nothing but glare at me." She shuddered.

"Sounds creepy."

"I ran out of there to the garage and drove off." She brushed strands of hair from her cheek. "I don't know where he went, if he's still out there."

"You poor thing." Karensa hugged her. "Do you think he's one of your neighbors?"

Gabrielle shrugged. "I suppose it's possible. I don't know any of my neighbors. The closest one is half a mile away." Her gaze fell on the scattered remnants from last night's fire in the hearth. "He sure didn't look friendly."

"Doesn't sound like it." Karensa got up from the couch. "How about that tea?"

"The pot is on the stove." She followed Karensa into the kitchen.

Ten minutes later, they sat at the wooden table in the kitchen with their steaming mugs of tea.

"You haven't brought up Jordan. No progress in that department?" Karensa raised her perfectly shaped onyx eyebrows.

"I brought him home last night. He was very sick, coughing and sweating with fever."

"Wow. So he came willingly?"

"Not exactly. But he was in no condition to argue with me."

"Good." Karensa grinned. "He should listen to you."

"He was gone when I got up this morning. I suppose he made it back to town. It's only five miles from here." She frowned. "I doubt he was totally well though."

"Probably not."

Leaning back in the chair, she slid her hand into her slacks pocket and felt the folded-up papers from Andrew. "Oh." She pulled them out and flattened them on the table's surface. "I found these in Andrew's clothes last night."

Karensa reached over and took them. With a puzzled expression, she read the letter.

"I don't know what he and *J* are talking about," Gabrielle said. "I've never seen these or heard Andrew say anything about them."

Karensa set the papers on the table. "It sounds like he was talking about you."

"I'm wondering what that surprise was." *Andrew, what were you concocting?*

"Of course you are."

"But I'm thinking the *J* stands for Jordan."

"Sounds right to me."

Gabrielle nodded.

Karensa smiled. "So, not only can you help Jordan, he can help you too."

But would he? Gabrielle hugged herself.

5

Gabrielle woke with a start, squinting at her surroundings. Shafts of morning light streamed through the sides of her closed blinds. The lamp on the nightstand beamed yellow. She'd left it on overnight after waking twice from nightmares of the creepy forest man. The sleeping pills were no longer working. Just as well. She'd wanted to get off the medicine months ago, and now she would. She couldn't afford to be doped up in the middle of the night with that man near her house. Yet she wouldn't let him obstruct her plans. Jordan needed her help.

The *J* written in Andrew's note had to be Jordan. She'd find out today if Jordan showed up at the parking lot. If he did, would he have recovered from his illness so soon?

SATURDAY AFTERNOON, Gabrielle drove down the street that led to her office and spied Jordan walking on the sidewalk with his hands in his pockets, face buried in the collar of his jacket, staring at the ground.

She rolled down the window. "Jordan!"

He turned at the sound of her voice, peeking sideways from his jacket. He waved and kept walking toward the opening to the parking lot of her work building. She stepped on the gas pedal and quickly turned the car into the lot and parked. As she exited the vehicle, Jordan crossed the lot to the adjoining sidewalk on the other side.

The crisp, icy air brushed her face as she jogged toward him. "Jordan!" Her breath puffed out in cottony clouds.

Thankfully, Jordan stopped and pivoted around as she approached him.

"I need to talk to you."

"Okay, talk." He buried his head in his coat's collar again but not before she caught sight of his face, which had returned to his regular shade, with no signs of fever.

"You look like you're feeling better."

"Yep. All better." He popped his head up. "Thanks for the other night."

She began to understand his pattern of behavior. Her question about his leaving early now seemed a waste of breath. "I'm glad I was able to help."

He nodded, then swiveled his head in the direction he was going.

She caught his arm. "I need to talk to you about Andrew."

He stared at the ground with his face pinched. "Haven't talked to somebody by now?"

She shook her head. "That's not what I mean. I need your help with something he wrote."

He glanced at her. "Like what?"

"Would you just tell me if you'll help me?"

"Don't know if I can."

"I think you can."

He blew out a breath and stared ahead. "Okay, but not right now. I'm going to the soup kitchen."

"We can go over to the café on the corner." She pointed in the direction from which she'd come.

"No, thanks. You're not going to pay for my meal." He sauntered down the sidewalk.

She pursed her lips. He was hell-bent on making her work even harder for his help. "Could you meet me back here at four?" She trotted after him.

"See you later." He flapped his hand and continued on.

Stubborn to the core. That was hardly a hurdle. She could and would match his stubbornness.

GABRIELLE SPOTTED Jordan standing by the opening to the parking lot across from her office, and she drove over and parked by the curb. She climbed out and walked toward him.

"Hello," she said.

"Hey."

"Would you mind coming to my house to talk?"

"You have a problem talking here?"

"The letters are at home."

"Letters?"

"Yes. Can we just go?"

He shrugged and followed her to her car.

When they stepped into her house, he stood by the door until she waved him into the living room. "Sit down. I'll get the papers."

While he ambled to the sofa, she shed her jacket, ran upstairs to retrieve the notes, and came back down just as quickly. She joined him on the couch.

She set the opened letters on the coffee table in front of them. "Here's the first one. I believe it's your message to him." She pointed to the *J* in the signature, then ran her finger over the second letter. "And this is his response to you."

Jordan studied the handwriting. "Yeah, I remember this now, but I never got his letter back... Until now." He picked up Andrew's note. "He wrote to me last April. I remember 'cause my girlfriend had just broken up with me. She moved to Reading for a new job."

"Only a month before his death." Her throat closed as she blinked back tears. *Not now.* She needed to keep focused.

He tapped the letter written by him. "Yeah. This was my answer."

She nodded.

"What it was about just came back to me," Jordan said, scratching his hairy chin.

She straightened up. "What does it mean?"

He glanced at her and chuckled with a hint of ruefulness in it. "He was planning something for your anniversary."

"Our anniversary?" Their wedding day popped into her head —an image of Andrew and her standing in front of the royal doors and altar, with *stefana* circling their heads. They were married June 25, with burgeoning, colorful flowers blanketing the grass surrounding the church. They would have celebrated eight years together.

"He wanted it to be a surprise." Jordan's whiskered face bunched up in the beginnings of a smile that turned downward as his brows met. He wagged his shaggy head.

My sweet Andrew. She smiled. "Well, he definitely accomplished that, because I never had a clue he was planning anything."

Jordan turned to face her. "He was planning your honeymoon."

"We didn't have one." She swallowed. "We couldn't afford it."

Andrew had started a new job at the local middle school,

and her parents at the time were struggling financially because of medical bills due to her father's declining health. They'd made a promise for a belated honeymoon that never came to fruition.

Jordan set his hand on top of hers that were clasped in her lap. "I'm sorry. I know this isn't easy for you."

Wiping a stray tear from under her eye, she inhaled deeply and exhaled slowly, working to calm herself.

"He loved you more than I've ever seen any man love a woman." Jordan patted her hand, then pointed at the note. "It's funny the letter was still with him. Probably a reminder to him to work on it."

"Work on it?"

"He was saving up money for the trip."

"Trip?"

"Yeah, to Belize."

She froze, astounded. But she shouldn't have been. That was where they'd wanted to go, to bask in the sun on the bright ivory beaches, their feet in the sand and cold drinks in their hands. But she'd believed it was a pipe dream. They'd always struggled to save the money to make it happen. Just this summer, she'd finally made a noticeable dent in Andrew's student loan by scaling down the amount to less than ten thousand.

"How'd he save up money? We never—"

"He managed to. Said he'd been saving twenty dollars here, thirty dollars there, out of his paychecks for about three years. He'd been planning it for a long time."

The revelation rocked her, making her light-headed. "I had no idea." But then she'd remembered how frugal he'd been since they married. Choosing to stay home instead of eating out more often than not and turning down several events, preferring to use the money to pay down debts. She remembered those few times his thriftiness had been irritating when she'd wanted so much to go to the theater to see a Broadway show or watch one of their favorite bands perform at a local venue in town. "Where'd he put the money?"

Jordan shrugged. "He didn't say exactly, only that he had stashed it in a safe place in the house."

Stunned again, her mouth fell open.

He chuckled. "He must have picked a stellar hiding place."

"Incredible hiding place." Gabrielle looked around the living room. Where would Andrew have hidden their money?

Jordan rose from the couch. "Got to go. The shelter is open now, and the cots go fast."

She tugged on his sleeve like a child. "Why can't you stay here tonight?"

He looked down at her with a furrowed brow. "You know why. I told you that the first day you saw me in the parking lot." He skirted the table and walked toward the door. "I'm not going to be a burden."

"But you're not. You're family." She stood up from the sofa and headed his way.

He gave her a deadpan expression. "I can walk back to town if you don't want to drive me."

She sighed. "No. I'll drive you back to the shelter."

After he climbed out of the car, Gabrielle watched him walk away. Then something clicked in her brain. Karensa had been right. He needed her help, and she needed his. But she'd have to find a way to persuade him that he was needed. And she would.

6

Sunday on her way home from church, Gabrielle's cell phone rang.

"Hey," Karensa said in a raspy voice. "I'm not feeling well. Got a nasty head cold."

"You poor thing." Gabrielle frowned as she turned the car onto the gravel driveway to her house.

Karensa sneezed. "So, we won't be able to meet up tonight. Hopefully, next week some time."

"No problem. I'll be in touch."

Her friend's unexpected cancelation of their get-together gave Gabrielle the chance to drive around town in search of Jordan.

After circling the Lancaster streets with no sight of Jordan, she headed home. She parked her car in the garage, then walked to the back door. By the elm, something stirred out of the corner of her eye. She turned, and a scream lodged in her throat. The intimidating forest man lurked near the bench and glowered at her before lumbering off toward the copse of trees.

With trembling hands, Gabrielle rattled the house key in the door's lock before it clicked open, and she ran in, slamming the door behind her. She turned the dead bolt and let out a shaky sigh.

Either this man is a nosy neighbor, or he's... She swallowed, thinking about what he could be doing in her backyard. Twenty feet away, those steely gray eyes filled with contempt had drilled into her. She shuddered, then grabbed her phone from her purse. She tapped in the number for the police station, then paused. What good would it do to tell them a creepy guy was lurking around her property? They wouldn't be able to do anything about it. The police only showed up if somebody broke into a person's house or some other real emergency.

Knowing this did nothing to calm her worries.

LATER IN THE AFTERNOON, dressed in jeans, a bulky sweater, and loafers, Gabrielle drove down Ballard Street, toward the homeless shelter, in search of Jordan. It didn't take long to spot him leaning against the stucco building that housed the homeless. A group of people were gathered by its closed doors. She parked by the curb near the building, scrambled out of the car, and strode toward Jordan. Just before she reached him, he looked up.

"Gabby." He ran a hand through his hair.

"Hey." She gestured toward the front doors. "Waiting for them to open?"

"Yep."

The air had grown colder that afternoon, and they stood with hunched shoulders.

For a moment, she hesitated to ask him to come home with her. She knew he'd make a fuss.

"So, what are you doing here?"

She gave him a weak smile. "You know, I'm still offering the extra bedroom."

"Yeah, I know, but in a few hours, the doors will open, and a cot will be mine for the night."

His sapphire eyes sparkled as if telling her he liked this routine, but she didn't believe him. She'd gotten accustomed to his prideful behavior, and she'd take this chance to show him she needed him.

"You said you'd help me find Andrew's present."

"I did?" The side of his mouth lifted in an amused smile.

"Come on." She'd have to be more convincing. "You know Andrew would want you to."

He frowned, then blew out a white puff of air. "What time is it?"

She looked at her wristwatch. "It's ten after three."

"The shelter opens at six. Guess I've got some time."

"Plenty."

GABRIELLE SKIPPED THE BEDROOM—IT was too obvious a place for Andrew to store the money. They started searching in the attic, still bundled in their coats. There wasn't any heating up there, and the draft had them giving off icy breaths. Several packed-up boxes, a folded-up card table, four chairs, and two paintings rested against the angled wooden walls. Two Rubbermaid containers of Christmas ornaments and decorations sat next to them.

"Don't think he would've stashed the money in one of those boxes," Jordan said, standing with his hands on his hips, looking at a pyramid of six brown containers.

"You're probably right."

She stepped over to the oil paintings of rural landscapes.

Maybe Andrew taped the money to the back of the artwork, like in movies where safes were located behind pictures mounted on walls. A spark of excitement coursed through her. There was something thrilling about this, like a treasure hunt—a treasure Andrew had meant for them to enjoy together. Excitement drained from her body.

Frowning, Gabrielle picked up the paintings and examined them. Nothing was tacked to their backsides or behind them. Only dust bunnies sat on the worn floor. She sighed.

Jordan peeked in the Christmas boxes, then turned toward her. "Nothing in those."

She hugged herself against the chilly air.

He shook his head with a furrowed brow. "The attic doesn't work for me. Andy wouldn't stow away money up here." He descended the stairs.

She followed him. "How about some tea?"

"Sounds good."

While she set up the teapot and mugs, Jordan sat at the wooden table. His shabby clothes appeared more faded than when she'd first seen them, and his tangled and wild beard matched the condition of his hair.

"Are those the only clothes you have?"

"No. Aside from the couple of jeans, shirts, and underwear in my backpack, I keep my Giorgio Armani wardrobe tucked away in my mansion off Marietta Avenue."

She grinned and crossed her arms. Stubborn *and* a smartass. Andrew never told her about this side of his favorite cousin. "Ha ha."

He shrugged and gave her a lopsided smile. "Yeah. These are it."

"Makes it tough for job interviews."

"Tough? Impossible." He grimaced.

She pictured him in a navy-blue suit, all cleaned up. "I think you and Andrew are about the same size."

He glanced down at his worn jeans and old jacket. "Yeah, we are. We borrowed each other's jeans and shirts a few years back."

"Would you watch the pot on the stove while I go upstairs for a moment?"

"Sure."

Andrew had owned three suits he wore to church and special events at his school—one black, one navy blue, and one charcoal gray. She opened the closet doors and pulled out the navy-blue suit, put the blazer to her nose and breathed in the faint scent left by him. She lovingly ran her hand over its sleeves and swallowed hard.

Gabrielle set the clothes on the bed. He hadn't had it dry-cleaned since the last time he wore it. *I hope the smell of him never fades from this house.* She wiped her wet cheeks.

Returning to the closet, she selected one of Andrew's ties—the yellow one—and a pair of his black dress shoes. A white shirt would complete the ensemble. Andrew's white shirts were all hanging together to the left of his suits and trousers. She took one and closed the doors.

Gabrielle entered the kitchen. Jordan sat at the table with their mugs covered with saucers, steeping. He looked at the items in her arms.

"You didn't have to do that."

"You need something to wear." She hung them on the pantry door. "And you can use my shower to clean up."

He didn't answer, just took a sip of his tea.

Gabrielle paced toward the table, then sat down, wishing there was something else she could do.

A blurred shape from her left peripheral darted past the kitchen window. Catching her breath as her stare flicked to the glass pane, she half rose in her chair. Was it the forest man again?

"What's wrong?" Jordan straightened in his chair, looking toward the window.

She let out a nervous laugh. "I have this bizarre and scary neighbor. Well, I guess it's a neighbor of mine. They all live a half mile or so from my house."

"Go on." His eyes glued to hers, jaw set, as he leaned toward the tabletop.

"I saw him a few days ago for the first time, in the woods behind the house. I was looking for you that morning when you'd left my house after staying the night when you were sick."

He kept staring with furrowed brows and gave her a nod.

"I'd never seen him before then. He leered at me with such loathing, it really scared me." She glanced out the window again. "I ran back to the house, got in the car, and left for work."

"What'd he look like?"

She cringed. "He was dressed in dingy clothes with a ragged blue bandanna around his head. He looked like a vagabond."

"Blue bandanna... Sounds like a homeless guy..."

"My friend Karensa suggested he might be a neighbor."

"I doubt it." Jordan's gaze focused through the window on portions of her backyard. He moved to the back door.

Gabrielle crossed the floor and stopped behind him. "I found him by one of my elms after I got home from church this morning."

Jordan turned with a start. "What did he do?"

"Nothing. I ran inside and locked the door, and he walked back toward the woods." She hugged herself to stop a shudder.

Jordan placed his hands on her shoulders. "I can't stay here."

She looked up at him. "What? Why?"

Jordan dropped his hands to his sides and looked pained. He rubbed his forehead. "There's a guy I ran into at the shelter last month. He stole my wallet that had my last five dollars in it. I had nothing else in it, other than my license." He glanced at her with a grimace.

"Oh no. Do you think this guy is—"

He shook his head. "That's not all."

She hugged herself again.

"Because of that, when I hadn't eaten for two days, I saw him at the shelter and pilfered a silver ring he had in his knapsack. I hocked it for money to get something to eat and a pair of socks."

He'd stolen something, which wasn't right. But the forest guy had stolen from Jordan first. Still, did that make it right? An eye for an eye? She had never believed in that. It never led to reconciliation or ended the unhealthy cycle. Yet how could she judge his actions when he was hungry, needing the most basic sustenance to survive? And what about this homeless shelter they'd been in? "The guy in the woods is the homeless man from the shelter, isn't he?"

Jordan gave her a sharp nod. "The blue bandanna gave it away. It's not the shelter I've been going to lately but another one in Columbia."

Columbia was about five minutes from her house.

Her muscles tightened. "So, he's dangerous?"

"I don't know for sure. I've only seen him steal. But the wild look I saw in his eyes told me he'd been using."

"Drugs?" She wrung her hands.

"Yeah. Maybe meth. Don't know." Jordan glanced out the back door's window once more.

The haunting billboards of people on meth and how unpredictable and unstable they were invaded her mind. The lethal drug annihilated people's physical appearances. What did it do to their brains?

She gnawed on her bottom lip. She wanted to shove Jordan out the door, away from her house in hopes the dangerous man would leave her property, but at the same time, she wanted Jordan to stay to protect her from that maniac.

Jordan looked at her again, and it was as if he'd read her mind. "I need to leave. He's followed me here."

"What will he do to you if he catches up to you?"

He shrugged with apprehension filling his eyes. "I'm not sure, but I don't want you in the middle of this."

Without thinking, the words fell from her lips as she gazed at nothing. "I kind of am though, since he's seen me at least twice."

He squeezed her shoulder. "Sorry, Gabby. I never should've come to your home."

The gesture was so touching and gentle her heart tightened and swelled with empathy. Before she could think what to say, Jordan opened the door, jogged across the yard, and down the gravel driveway.

7

———

Gabrielle sat on Karensa's sofa with a cup of tea in her hand. "Jordan came into my life for a reason, and I believe that reason is to help him get back on his feet, career wise."

"I know, love, but now that you've filled me in about that creepy dude lurking in your backyard, I'm really worried for you." Karensa put a hand on Gabrielle's arm, her eyes soft with concern.

Gabrielle shut her eyes, pushing away thoughts about the man stalking Jordan. All she wanted was to help Andrew's cousin. The close bond Andrew and Jordan had connected her to them like a conduit.

"You're off inside your mind again," Karensa said.

"Sorry." She put the teacup on the coffee table. "Of course I understand your concern, but I have to... I need to help Jordan. I can't let Andrew down. He'd want me to help his cousin."

Karensa sighed. "That's right. You feel compelled to do this."

"Yes."

"So, what are you going to do?"

"I'll keep checking in with my HR director to see if maybe

something opens up at one of our satellite offices in the coming weeks."

"What if none come about?"

"I'll deal with that then. One thing at a time." Gabrielle leaned against the puffy cushions of the couch.

"Sorry to bring this up again, but it's really bothering me." Karensa grimaced. "This dangerous guy on drugs—"

"Jordan's not sure he's on drugs."

"—has been following Jordan and spending a lot of time in your backyard. Have any idea what to do about him?"

"Maybe Jordan will talk to him in town and settle their dispute."

"How? He stole the guy's ring."

"I don't know if that was even his ring. He stole money from Jordan. He could have stolen that ring from somebody else."

"Fair enough, but I'm not sure how Jordan can fix this problem."

"Neither am I, but there's got to be a way to resolve the feud and, at the same time, work on helping Jordan secure a job."

"Is Jordan on board with any of this?"

"Well, he doesn't know I'm wanting to work out a solution with him and the forest man, but I think he's open to my help on the job issue. He seemed to be okay with wearing Andrew's suit."

"He'll probably need a good shower before he puts it on." Karensa examined her fingernails, then looked at Gabrielle.

"Of course. And a shave, or at least trim his beard."

"Let's hope it's a shave."

Gabrielle shook her head and cracked a smile. Her friend never liked men with facial hair. "Whatever Jordan wants. It's his face."

Karensa shrugged.

"Do you have Friday off?"

"Yes. I may spend the day soaking in bath bombs." Karensa blew on the surface of her teacup, gazing as if in a dreamlike trance.

"As you should, considering all those crazy coworkers you deal with every day." Gabrielle chuckled.

Karensa snorted. "Who would've thought an office job could be so zany?"

She raised her hand. "I do, but in my case, it hasn't been as bad. There are always those cliques though."

"Yes, and they're maddening." Karensa set down her cup. "What are your plans for Thanksgiving?"

"I'll be at my parents' house."

"Good, love. You need to be around family. I know your mom and sister miss you."

"Angie is busy with her husband and kids." Gabrielle plucked imaginary lint off her black sweater.

"Not too busy for her sister, especially during the holidays, and you know darn well that's the truth." Karensa pursed her lips, nodding.

It was Gabrielle's turn to shrug.

"Your mom's going to be thrilled."

Gabrielle bit her lip. "I haven't visited her since early October."

Karensa leaned back against the cushions. "When your dad passed away, you were there for your mom. Let her be there for you. Try to enjoy the gathering."

"I will." Although she'd keep the forest man to herself while at her mother's.

"Gabrielle, dear, I'm so glad you came," her mother said. "The holiday wouldn't be the same without you here." Marcia kissed Gabrielle's cheek and gave her a warm embrace.

But Andrew was missing. Gabrielle returned her mother's hug for a long moment to collect herself. "It's only right after not stopping in for over a month."

Her mother put out her hands. "Let me have your coat and things. I'll set them—"

"I can do it. You go back into the kitchen with Angie. I'll be there in a sec."

Gabrielle removed her coat, scarf, and gloves and laid them on the bench by the front door. Above the seat hung a painting of cherubs in the foreground, floating above mountains crowned with clouds in the background. There were many other works of art in the house that depicted angels. Marcia collected angel paraphernalia. She loved them so much she'd named Gabrielle and her sister after them.

Another wave of heartache over Andrew's absence hit her. She smoothed out her sweater several times and took in a cleansing breath. She'd try to focus on her family, really listen and be helpful.

The small living room on the left side of the entrance was cloaked in shadows with the glimmer of soft light from the kitchen and den on the right, saving it from the void of any illumination. The scent of roasting turkey floated in the warm air.

After removing her shoes by the bench, Gabrielle made her way toward the drifting voices of Angie and her mother in the kitchen.

Angie's daughter trotted over to her as she entered the kitchen. "Hi, Aunt Gabby."

"Hey, Beth." She hugged her niece. "You've grown since the last time I saw you."

She hadn't seen Angie and her family since mid-August. They'd gotten together for a family cookout at their house. Gabrielle managed to make some of the family's gatherings since the beginning of the summer months but didn't remember much. She'd been there in physical form only. Her heart and mind were doused in grief. Just thinking about it caused her heart to clench. She pushed it from her mind, needing to be present.

She felt a hand on her arm. "I'm in fifth grade now."

"How are you liking it?"

Beth pursed her lips. "It's okay."

She chuckled. "Not too different from fourth grade, is it?"

Beth shook her head with a giggle and wandered out of the kitchen. The din of sportscasters gabbing on about football blared from the TV in the den. Gabrielle peeked in the living room and waved at Rod, Angie's husband, and Ben, her son. A commercial break burst from the TV, louder than the game. Rod and Ben exchanged hellos with her.

Gabrielle pivoted toward her mother and sister.

"Football season," Angie said in a listless tone.

"Of course." She parroted her sister's lack of enthusiasm.

"How's work going, dear?" Marcia asked as she stirred the pan of gravy.

"Same ol', same ol'."

"Sounds thrilling." Angie snickered and opened a cabinet by the fridge, pulling out plates.

Gabrielle shrugged. "That's how it goes in the working world."

"Yeah, I remember it." Angie quit working outside the home after giving birth to her firstborn, Ben. She took the plates through an arched entry to the dining room.

Gabrielle washed her hands in the sink, then opened the

utensil drawer and pulled out the needed items before walking into the dining room.

"So, anything else going on in your life besides work?" Angie asked as they worked together setting dishes and utensils on the mahogany table.

Without thinking, the words poured out of her mouth. "I'm helping Andrew's cousin, Jordan, find a job. He's homeless."

Angie stopped folding the napkin in her hand and stared at Gabrielle, her mouth ajar. "Homeless?"

"Yes. He lost his job, and his jerk of a roommate kicked him out of their apartment four months ago."

"Wow. He's not in trouble... I mean, with drugs or anything?"

Angie's first thought assumed Jordan was a drug addict, which wasn't surprising, really. She had a tendency to see the worst in just about every situation. She'd jump to negative conclusions whenever there was something going on in a family member or friend's life. Maybe being a mother made Angie more protective and guarded. Gabrielle's memories of trying to conceive a child flashed through her mind. She squeezed her eyes shut and blotted out the images.

"Gabby?"

She concentrated on what Angie had said. "Of course not. He lost his job, and that led to not having the money to pay for rent, and so he was evicted. It could happen to anyone."

"Yes, I'm sure it could." Angie resumed her task of folding napkins and placing them on the table next to each plate but then paused again. "Do you really think it's a good idea to be taking on such an ordeal when you've already gone through so much the past few months?"

The older, authoritative sister had kicked in. Gabrielle was used to Angie's analyzing her choices, but this one stung. For months, Gabrielle didn't see a reason to live without Andrew. Everything had become a blur, meaningless. It had taken all she had to return to work with a smile pasted on her face, prodding herself to do her job. Finding Jordan in the parking lot that day had been a wake-up call. Terrible things happened in life. Yet people were to keep going, finding a reason to.

"Not at all. I like being able to help somebody, especially family."

"I guess he's family." Angie walked back to the kitchen.

She followed Angie and took the glasses she handed her. "You guess? Jordan is Andrew's cousin."

"Sure, I understand." Carrying the last three glasses, Angie trailed behind her as they returned to the dining room and set down the cups by each plate.

"I'm glad."

Angie peered at her from across the table. "But I think it's an extra burden to take on when you're still mourning."

"I don't see it that way." She put her hands on her hips.

"I know you don't. You've always been naive. You want to help people but don't think it through, like with a homeless man. It could cause problems."

"I don't think—"

"You haven't been thinking straight since Andrew's death."

Gabrielle smoothed out a napkin with shaky hands as the familiar ache of grief rolled through her.

"I've seen it for a while now, how you walk around with an empty look." Angie shook her head, her brow furrowed. "I don't want to see you go through more pain when you can't fix this guy's problems."

Marcia stood at the doorway with her arms folded across her chest. "Fix what guy's problems? And what are his problems?"

Gabrielle combed her fingers through her hair, working, again, to brush aside the familiar pain of Andrew's loss. She hadn't really wanted to go into any of this. She knew she'd get what she'd just received from Angie and her mother. She didn't want to cause her worry. *Stupid.* Not thinking before she spoke was a nasty habit of hers.

"Gabby is helping Jordan, a homeless guy. She wants to help him get a job, although I really don't know how she's going to do that," Angie answered before she could.

Gabrielle cringed at her mother's pale face as she crossed herself. She had to stifle the impulse to answer in Jordan's defense. It would only keep this unfruitful conversation going. "Let's not talk about this now. I'm sorry I brought it up. Can we just enjoy Thanksgiving without arguing?"

Angie held up her palms. "Who's arguing? I'm just concerned about you, that's all."

"I have to take the turkey out, but I'd like to hear more about this later." Marcia turned on her heel and walked back into the kitchen.

"Hopefully, not while we're eating," Gabrielle said.

"After dinner," Angie suggested.

"That's fine with me," Marcia said as she pulled out the covered baking pan and set it on the stove.

AFTER DINNER, Gabrielle, Angie, and their mother gathered in the kitchen.

"All right, Gabrielle. What is Angela in a tither about?" Marcia asked, raising her thin brows.

"Mother, I'm not in a tither, just concerned." Angie scowled as she dumped the plates in the sink filled with soapy water.

Marcia stacked the remaining dishes to be washed. "Fine, dear. Let's see what Gabrielle has to say." She waved a hand in Gabrielle's direction.

Gabrielle regretted having ever brought up Jordan. Chiding herself again, she plowed forward, making sure to leave out any parts that would be worrisome to her mother. "It's nothing, really. I'm just helping Jordan find a job since he lost his six months ago."

"Lost his job *and* his apartment *and* is *living on the streets*," Angie threw out in the middle of their partial circle.

Marcia turned from the faucet, her hands finding her hips. "Well, that's just awful for Jordan. Poor man."

Angie gaped. "Of course, but do you really think it's a good idea for Gabby to be getting involved with a man who lives on the streets? Who knows what riffraff he hangs around with because of his circumstances?"

Gabrielle hadn't even brought up the creepy guy stalking Jordan, but that didn't seem to matter. Angie managed to conjure up her own story.

Marcia smiled, as if unaffected by Angie's remarks. "I'm sure your sister wouldn't get involved with riffraff, dear. Besides, helping a friend—"

"And family member," Gabrielle interjected.

Marcia's eyes flicked to her. "Yes. Helping a family member or friend in need is a good thing."

Angie, with pursed lips, pivoted toward the sink and scrubbed a soapy plate. "Just watching out for my little sister," she mumbled.

Marcia put a hand on Angie's shoulder. "Of course, dear. We all are." She then looked back at Gabrielle with a gentle grin. "It's good to have someone to help, especially this time of year."

"Yes, but doesn't she have enough on her plate? Why not get involved in a stress-free activity at church or start up a nice hobby like knitting? Something less... less risky?"

"Risky? What's risky about searching online jobs for Jordan?" their mother asked, taking a towel and drying the cup Angie set on the dish rack.

Before Angie could respond, Gabrielle cut in. "That's right.

What risk is it for me to check online and at my office to see if there are any openings?" She preferred her mother's presumption of how she was helping Jordan, for her sake.

Angie grunted. "Nothing, I guess."

"Then there's nothing for any of us to worry about." Marcia affectionately patted Angie's back before returning a glass to its rightful spot in the cupboard.

Gabrielle nodded. She'd managed to convince her mother there was nothing to fear. Now she just needed to convince herself.

8

___

Gabrielle left her office, the bitter cold breeze slicing through her. She peered at the large garbage container through the curtain of dusk that had fallen over the city. The details around the dumpster were hard to make out. She tucked her chin below her scarf and moved closer in search of Jordan.

Halfway behind the dumpster lay a crumpled figure facing away from her. Gabrielle pulled out her mobile phone and shined its light over the body. Recognizing the gray jacket, she sucked in a breath.

"Jordan!"

She bent down and touched his shoulder, then ran the light over the crown of his head. No blood or noticeable injuries. She focused the beam on his face, mottled with bruises and blood. "Oh no." She gently shook his shoulder. "Jordan."

He twitched, then slowly moved. "Uhhh."

Thank God! She swept back his hair from his beaten face. "Can you get up?"

His blue eyes blazed through indigo slits in his puffy face. "Y-yeah, I think so." He labored to sit up.

She gently pulled on his arm to help him to his feet.

He grumbled something unintelligible as he took clumsy steps forward as if he were drunk.

"Let me help you." She wrapped her arm around his waist, then scanned the ground. "Where's your backpack?"

"Gone."

He had nothing now. She bit her lip and led him to her car.

He didn't protest as she opened the car door for him. He collapsed onto the seat and winced. His lip split open, oozing out blood.

Gabrielle fumbled in her purse for a tissue and handed it to him.

With eyes shut, his hand bumped into hers, and she shoved the tissue into his palm.

Hastily she slid into the driver's side seat and started the car.

SLAMMING the back door to her home and locking it, she helped guide Jordan into the living room to the couch. He fell onto the cushions, grunting out profane words. She spread the afghan over his body.

Gabrielle ran around the house, gathering painkillers, gauze wraps, wound ointments, and a glass of water. Returning to the living room with the items, she began to work on his face.

"Ugh," he said as his lip continued to dribble blood.

"I'm going to clean your face with this warm washcloth." She blotted the blood from his nose and mouth. "But I should have taken you to the hosp—"

"No. Can't afford it," he said, his voice hoarse. "And neither can you."

She sighed. Even if she offered, he wouldn't allow her to pay.

He said nothing more while she continued nursing him. He fell asleep before she could administer the pain medication.

She left the ointment and gauze on the table and hung the washcloth in the downstairs bathroom. When she passed by the prayer shelf, she touched the icon of archangel Gabriel sitting on the rack. "Please help him."

Below the shelf, the oil and wick were out in the vigil lamp. She replaced them, lit a match, and a new flame flickered to life.

She picked up Andrew's picture and kissed his face. "My love, pray for your cousin."

GABRIELLE SET A PLATE OF EGGS, sausage, and a blueberry bagel in front of Jordan, followed by a cup of orange juice. He sat at the kitchen table next to the window, as the fingers of dawn laced through the blackened sky.

"Eat," she said and stuffed a chunk of blueberry bagel in her mouth while clicking across the tile floor in her black pumps.

"Yeah, yeah." He flapped a hand at her. His multicolored face winced as he opened his mouth slowly to slide in a forkful of scrambled eggs.

She hated having to go to work today. He still needed more time to heal, and she knew he'd be gone by the time she came home in the evening. She sat across from him. "I don't need to ask who did that to you."

"Nope." Jordan continued eating with a grimace.

"What happened?"

He set down his fork and glanced up at her through swollen black lids. "He must've followed me down one of the streets near the shelter. Caught me by surprise. Kept asking me where the ring was. I told him I didn't have it, that I sold it. He didn't believe me. Beat the shit out of me." Jordan sniffed and picked up his fork. "And took my backpack for good measure."

"He walloped you good, Jordan. What happens the next

time he finds you? What will he do to you then?" Worry snaked through her stomach. "What can be done to stop him?"

He looked at her with wariness. "Nothing."

"Not what I wanted to hear," she said with a raised brow. "There's got to be something."

"Like what?"

Ideas wouldn't come. Jordan wouldn't be able to contain the guy long enough for the police to arrest him. She rubbed her forehead. "So you're just supposed to be a sitting duck, waiting to be hurt again, or worse?"

He set his fork down once more and pushed his dish away. "I'm not sure what I'm supposed to do. But since he seems to know my every move, you know I can't stay here."

She clenched her teeth. "Yes, I know. Because it's not safe for me." She wasn't going to settle for being helpless. There had to be something she could do, but what?

"That's right. For Andrew, I can't let you get any more involved than you already are. It's bad enough this guy knows where you live." He stood slowly, putting a hand to his ribs. "As long as I stay away from your house, I think he'll leave you alone. After all, he doesn't want you; he wants me."

This guy was willing to pound Jordan into sand for the wedding band. "I wonder if that was his wedding ring." She tapped the table's wooden surface. "Maybe he lost his wife."

Jordan ran a hand through his greasy, disheveled hair. "He's not going to tell me, and even if he did, how would that change anything? I don't have it anymore."

She looked at him. "Maybe you could go to that pawn shop and get it back."

He stared at her, his slatted eyes widening. "How do I get it back, Gabby? With what?" He tugged on his top. "My shirt?"

She rose from her chair and headed to the living room to

grab her coat. "I could help out. How much can an old ring cost?"

"I got thirty dollars for it." Jordan walked to the couch and, bending over gingerly, picked up his jacket. "But I won't let you pay for it."

"Thirty dollars. That's not much. Must not be real gold." She ran her fingers over her gold wedding band.

"It was silver, and it sure helped me get a couple of cheap meals and an extra pair of socks."

"The socks that were probably in your backpack."

"Yeah."

Gabrielle frowned. "You need socks... clothes."

"I'll figure out how to get some."

"How are you going to do that?" She folded her arms across her chest.

"I'll think of something. I can be resourceful."

"You mean like when you stole the hostile homeless man's ring and hocked it for money? That worked out well."

"Hey, I got food out of it." He cracked a smile, then moaned, touching his red lip.

Gabrielle rolled her eyes. "You know you can't go that route again. Look at you." She picked up a tube of lip balm off the coffee table. "Here, take this with you. It'll help that lip heal."

He took it from her hand and dabbed it on. "Thanks," he said, looking around. "Thanks for everything."

"You're welcome." She glanced at him. "Is there any way I can convince you to come back this evening? Give you one more night to rest and recover before you're out for good?"

He shook his head. "I just told you it's not safe for you."

He was being extra stubborn and overprotective, but his behavior seemed to be a natural trait. Andrew had been the same way. She sucked on her bottom lip, tempering the ache inside her.

His stare softened. "If I know the guy isn't following me here, I'll try to come back tonight." He raised his finger and wagged it. "But just tonight."

"Of course." She laced her fingers together. Maybe he wasn't *that* stubborn.

9

———

After work, Gabrielle drove Jordan to the pawnshop where he'd hocked the ring.

Jordan sat with his hands in his coat pockets in the passenger seat. "You know, there's no guarantee it's still there. The guy could have sold it by now."

"Yes, I know." She parked the car, and they headed to the front door of the dilapidated building with a flashing neon-pink OPEN sign in its barred window.

They entered the store, empty of people other than a man who looked to be in his sixties, standing behind an ancient register. His graying broom mustache hid his lips. His eyes followed them as they approached. Strangely enough, he didn't so much as blink at the sight of Jordan with his bruised face and fat lip.

"Can I help you?" he said in a cheerful voice.

She gave a sideways glance to Jordan.

"Yeah. I sold you a ring about a month or so ago."

The man drummed his fingers on the counter. "You're gonna have to be more specific. I get rings of all kinds all the time."

"It was a simple silver band, like a wedding ring."

"Get lots of those too. Men, women change their minds and dump them here."

Gabrielle shifted from one foot to the other. This wasn't going to be as easy as she thought. "It was a man's silver band—"

"And you gave me thirty dollars for it," Jordan added.

He eyed them while scratching his chin. "Hmmm." He waved a hand and lumbered toward a metal-and-glass case on his right. "All my rings are in this case. If it ain't here, it's been sold."

They moved to the case with three shelves of rings. A few looked like gold, some silver, and some sported large gems. The tiny price tags below them held huge dollar amounts.

The man tapped the glass with an index finger. "Them rings over there are wedding bands."

Three rows of gold, silver, copper, and titanium rings gleamed back at them.

Gabrielle looked in Jordan's direction. "Do you see it?"

He continued to examine the selection. "The ring didn't look as good as these."

The owner grunted out a cough. "I always polish 'em up before putting 'em out for customers." He wiped his mouth with a handkerchief.

Jordan grimaced as he pushed away from the glass. "I don't know. I don't see it."

Disappointment set in but only for a moment. "Why can't we just buy one and give it to the guy?"

He shook his head. "He'd know it wasn't his... The one he had."

"So, he gets a better one," she said, laying a hand on Jordan's arm.

"Look at the prices, Gabby." Jordan jerked a thumb toward the racks of jewelry.

She shrugged. "We get an affordable one."

"You mean like the dull silver one for two hundred dollars?" Jordan asked, with one eyebrow raised above his bloated eye.

Her stare shot to the rings again. "Two hundred dollars?" She gaped.

The pawnbroker sniffed. "It's real silver."

"It's a rip-off," Jordan retorted.

"You don't like it, go someplace else. I gotta make a livin', you know?"

Jordan straightened himself, and with his jaw clenched, glared at the man. "Good idea." He turned to leave, but Gabrielle caught his arm.

"Hold on," she whispered.

"What?" Jordan answered gruffly. He gave another angry look at the man wiping the glass countertop with his handkerchief. "He paid thirty bucks for the silver ring I gave him. I'm not going to let you pay this swindler that outrageous amount." He'd raised his voice.

"Shh." She patted his chest and glanced over Jordan's shoulder. "Maybe we can bargain with him."

"Didn't you just hear him? He's not going to budge."

"I want to try."

With an exasperated expression, he focused his eyes on the door.

"Please."

He sighed. "You're wasting your time, but do what you want."

"Mr.... Ah, I'm sorry. What is your name?" she asked.

"Floyd. That's what I go by."

"Hi, Floyd. I'm Gabby." She stuck out her hand.

Floyd slipped the cloth from his right hand into his left and shook hers. "Nice to meet you." He grinned large, coffee-stained teeth at her.

She gazed at the silver wedding band, then at her own. She

spread her fingers and showed Floyd her wedding ring on her right hand. "This is my wedding ring. I never take it off."

He brought up the glasses dangling on a chain around his neck and perched them halfway down his nose. "It's real nice." He bobbed his head once at her, his face wrinkling in appreciation.

"Thank you."

His bushy brows came together. "Why ain't your wedding ring on your left hand?"

"It's my family's tradition to wear it on our right hands."

"Ah. Gotcha." He nodded. "Do you wanna add to that with one of them nice diamond or ruby rings?" Floyd squinted at her. "Naw... the emerald. It goes with your eyes." He fished in his trousers pocket for something and pulled out a round key chain with two keys hanging from it.

"Oh no. That's all right, Floyd," she said, waving a hand at him. "It's a beautiful ring, but I'm not interested in getting any of those. I only wear this one. I can't imagine wearing any other ring on my hand since he's gone."

Floyd's face flushed. "Gone and left ya, huh? The jerk."

Jordan stiffened next to her, raising his arm. Afraid he'd strike the man, she grabbed his arm.

Letting out a nervous laugh, she said, "No, he didn't leave me... at least not in the way you mean."

Floyd puckered his lips. "Left you for another guy?"

"Oh no. I just mean my husband reposed six months ago."

"Reposed?" He eyed her above his reading glasses. "What's that?"

"He died," Jordan interjected with a frustrated sigh.

Floyd's mouth fell open. "Oh. I'm... I'm sorry. That's a real shame."

"Thank you." She pointed to the silver ring they'd been looking at. "My husband's ring was silver like that one, and he was buried wearing it. Do you think I could get that silver ring to wear around my neck? It would be comforting having that hanging near my heart."

"You bet." He jammed the key into the cabinet's lock and slid the partition to the side. He snatched out the ring and set it on the glass top. "See how it catches the light?"

Gabrielle craned her neck to get a closer look. "Yes, I do."

"It's durable for hangin' on a chain around your neck too."

"That's great, Floyd." She picked up the ring and examined it. "Gee, I don't have a lot of money to spend. It's just me, and I don't make that much."

"Aww, well, I can let you have it for a hundred bucks."

"One hundred dollars?" She frowned. "I'm afraid it's not in my budget."

Floyd's mouth worked as if he was determined to barter with her now. She peered at Jordan out of the corner of her eye. He stood speechless with his puffy eyes as wide as they could open.

Floyd slapped the glass counter. "Never mind one hundred. What was I thinking? This one is on sale for... for seventy-five bucks."

"Seventy-five dollars." Jordan smirked, rolling his eyes.

"It's a good deal. My final—"

"I'll take it," she blurted out and dug in her purse.

"Gab—"

"Hush." She pulled out her debit card and handed it to Floyd, who was beaming.

"You got a deal today. This little piece of jewelry is a real good buy," Floyd rattled on as he rang up her card through a more modern contraption than his archaic register.

"I did. Thank you so much." She took her card from him, then thrust out her other hand on which Floyd set the little felt box with the ring inside.

"You're welcome. Don't forget to tell 'em who sold you the ring," he said as they walked out of the store.

68

10

—————

When they entered her home, guilt bit Gabrielle over having used Andrew's death to talk the pawnshop owner down in price. But she'd had no other option. In front of the prayer shelf, she made the sign of the cross. *Forgive me.* She lit a fresh wick on the oil-filled kandelia.

Jordan sat on the couch, holding the ring box. "I hope this works."

He'd come back with her. Maybe she was wearing down his stubbornness after all. She switched on the bear lamp, then padded to the hearth and started a fire.

"It should." She sat down on the glider, closed her eyes, and leaned back against its soft cushion.

"Confronting him will be tricky. I'll have to make myself an easy target."

She sat upright. "Isn't that dangerous?"

He shrugged. "How else am I going to reach him? It's not like I can give him a call."

She leaned back in the chair again. There had to be a way to defuse the contention between the two men. A right way. "Maybe if you come to him humbly—"

"Humbly?" Jordan's face clouded. "Why would I do that for a thief?"

"Do you think he'll forgive you for stealing his ring?"

"We don't know for sure the ring even belonged to him."

"Suppose it did." She looked at him. "If you forgive him for taking—"

"Stealing."

"—your wallet, maybe he'll soften and leave you alone."

"Forgive him?" Jordan thumped a hand to his chest. "Why are you laying this on me?"

"Because you're a levelheaded, good guy. You've been on the streets for a few months now and have seen people suffering."

He only grunted in response.

For a long minute, silence took up the space between them.

Jordan sighed. "I'll search him out at the Columbia shelter tomorrow." He winced as he set down the ring box on the coffee table.

It reminded Gabrielle why she'd wanted him to stay the night. Recuperation. She got up from the glider and took the afghan from the top of the couch. "Come on. Lie down and rest. I'm going to make some tea and get you ibuprofen."

He stretched out on the sofa. She raised her brows. He'd actually done what she'd advised.

When she came down with the medicine and a cup of water, she said, "I'll be keeping my eye out for openings at work and search online when I have my lunch breaks."

"Okay." Jordan scooted up on the couch and took the cup and pills.

She headed into the kitchen for their tea. When she returned to the living room, Jordan was staring intently at the orange flames in the fireplace.

"Things are changing, Gabby." He held up the jewelry box. "We now have a bargaining tool to get this guy off my back. And because of your help, I have clothes for interviewing. This'll give me a real chance at a job."

She sat again in the glider. "Good. That's what I'm aiming for."

It was as if something had truly changed in both of them. He showed optimism, and hope blossomed in her heart, a hope that saw life ahead as post grief and cherished memories. Andrew's letter came to mind. She was determined more than ever to find his gift for her. Nothing could sever their union, not even death. They were eternally united. She smiled, feeling a new purpose and contentment she hadn't felt since before Andrew's repose.

"As soon as my face doesn't look like it's been mauled, I'll clean up and get to job searching." Jordan leaned his head on the couch's arm.

She'd never seen Jordan in such a positive mood and hoped this attitude would stay with him.

In the cozy room full of shadows dancing on the walls as the fire blazed in the hearth, Jordan fell asleep. *Yes, things were changing for the better.* With a smile, Gabrielle passed the humble twinkle of light gleaming from the suspended oil lamp on her way to bed.

SOMETHING SHATTERED DOWNSTAIRS. Gabrielle shot up in bed, pressing a palm to her chest, her heart sprinting inside. Fear seeped through her bones as she slid out of bed.

She glanced at the picture of her and Andrew on the nightstand next to her cell phone. *What's happening downstairs?* Grabbing the mobile and shoving it into the pocket of her pajama bottoms, she went to the door. She gripped the knob, twisted it without a sound, and peeked through the crack.

The dark hallway was empty. She inched her way down the

corridor to the stairs. The sounds of scuffling and dragging something across the floor came from downstairs. Was Jordan moving around down there? Did he hurt himself, or was there someone else in the house with them? She caught her breath and pushed forward.

The subtle odor of stale cigarettes hung in the space, so faint she wasn't sure if it was real or imagined. Considering the shaky state she was in, she chalked it up to imagination.

When her foot settled on the second step down, the back door creaked. The dragging continued a minute more before the door shut with a clunk.

She crept down the rest of the stairs. The full moon's bright light flooded through the living room windows. Ahead of her, the kandelia swayed gently as a thin stream of smoke from the once-lit wick floated to the ceiling. The burnt smell drifted through the tepid air.

Where had Jordan gone?

Gabby tiptoed over to the swinging lamp. The glass was still half-full of oil. She glanced at archangel Gabriel. His gentle face gleamed in the moonlight while the rest of the wall was shrouded in shadows. Below the angel, Andrew's picture sat in darkness, with the vase of roses lying on its side, the flowers half out of the vase and some on the floor with water dripping off the edge of the table. *Oh no. Your roses.* She set the vase upright and put the flowers back inside the glass container.

Across from her on the floor lay her precious bear lamp broken in two, its quaint shade dented in several spots. She stepped over to the hearth where jagged pieces of a porcelain dish she'd had on the mantel lay on the fireplace brick and part of the area rug.

How had this happened? Her skin crawled. The forest man must have come back for Jordan.

The coffee table sat on its side, and the couch was pushed

back a foot. Near one of the table's legs was the unopened jewelry box from the pawnshop. She snatched it and pulled the lid open. The ring was still there. Maybe their skirmish robbed Jordan of the chance to give the man the ring. She'd give it to him, and he'd leave Jordan alone.

She peered out the window, then ran to the front door and jammed her feet into her winter boots. Jordan must have left through the back door. Yanking her coat from the peg, she stuffed her arms through the sleeves. She dropped the small box into one of her coat's deep pockets and clopped across the living room into the kitchen. A thin trail of blood droplets led to the back door.

Queasiness rolled through her stomach. *I hope that's not your blood, Jordan.* Gabrielle swallowed hard and glanced at the clock on the kitchen wall. Three thirty. It would be another three hours before daybreak. She'd have to search for them in the dark.

She bit her lip as her hand clasped the doorknob. Slowly she opened it. The icy wind rushed inside, slashing her face. She hugged her coat around her and stumbled onto the frost-laden yard.

The moon's beams, the back porch light, and two halogen lights on either end of the garage lit the path in front of her. Her car stood outside from the night before. Brown glistening drops on the ground led toward the garage. *Jordan, I'm on my way. Be okay, be okay...* She gritted her teeth as the breeze cut through her.

She reached the side door to the garage that was cracked open. The pungent smell of gasoline burned her nostrils. *Is something on fire?* She swung open the door and stepped into the darkened space. A shaft of moonlight landed on a battered, blood-splotched figure on the cement floor across from her.

Tears stung Gabrielle's eyes, blurring her vision. "Jordan!"

Something hard struck the back of her head. She collapsed into a black abyss.

11

Gabrielle woke coughing. Smoke invaded her lungs. She opened her eyes to the darkness around her and sat up. A jolt of pain pulsated from the back of her head. She rubbed it as her vision adjusted to her surroundings.

Through the gray clouds hovering around her, she spotted Jordan lying lifeless in the same place. *Is he dead?*

Heat permeated the space. Flames licked the wooden cabinet at the left corner of the room.

How am I going to get him out of here? Fear paralyzed her.

An angry red blaze shot through the broken window next to the hanging tools. Her eyes stung and watered as the thick fog smothered her, sending her into ragged hacking. The overpowering smell of gasoline and soot burned her nose. She got on all fours, trying to get below the billowing smoke.

A hard object weighed down her pajama pants pocket. She lifted her coat and stuck her hand into its pocket and pulled out her phone. Letting out a violent cough, she wheezed, fumbling with the mobile. Her lungs screamed, tight and constricted. Through tear-laden eyes, Gabrielle pushed its screen to bring up the call icon. Blinking away stinging moisture, she hit the numbers needed. With a last gasp for air, she hit the Send button before the ashy haze towed her under.

———

A BLINDING beam flickered over her eyelids as she felt her body jostle on a hard-stretched cloth. The cold air stung her face and sent a shiver through her.

"She's coming to," a man's voice said, and the bright light flashed over her lids again.

Gabrielle's eyes opened. The familiar ache in the back of her head pulsated. Two figures bent over her.

"Check her vitals," the same voice said.

"Hi, Ms. Vakis. I'm going to listen to your heart." The face of a woman came into focus with the ends of a stethoscope in her ears. She lowered a heavy blanket from Gabrielle's chest, unbuttoned the top of her pajama shirt, and gently pressed something cool against her left breast. The frosty air brushed her skin, making her shudder.

The glow of the back porch's yellow light colored their faces.

What happened to her? Where was Jordan?

Alarm raced through her like a bolt of lightning. She yelled "Jordan," but it only came out as a whisper from her dry lips through an oxygen mask covering her mouth and nose.

"I'm sorry. What did you say?" the woman asked, leaning toward Gabrielle and turning her head to the side.

"Jor— Jordan," she said in a raspy voice.

Gabrielle's throat was sore, her chest tight. She couldn't take a deep breath without coughing. The dusty, acrid smell of smoke wafted in the air. *Oh my god. The fire in the garage!*

She struggled to rise but couldn't.

"He's in the ambulance," the woman responded, rebuttoned

Gabrielle's pajama top, and pulled the blanket back over her chest.

Gabrielle looked past the two paramedics to their ambulance lined up next to another one, a fire truck, and a police car. Their headlamps and blue and red flashing lights streamed across the yard.

When the EMT finished checking her blood pressure, she willed herself to sit up, pushing against the flat cot on the ground as leverage. A dull ache thrummed at the lower back of her head. She groaned and raised her right hand to massage the sore spot but stopped. Her ring finger was bare. Chills ran through her as she brought her hand closer. "My wedding ring. It's gone..." Her lips quivered as her parched throat closed and eyes filled with tears.

"Whoa, calm down. It'll be okay. Here," the paramedic said and handed her a tissue.

Gabrielle scanned the ground around her. "Where's... where's my jacket?"

"Craig, bring her coat."

The male paramedic walked over to the hollowed metal frame that used to be the door to her garage. A blackened shell and several crumbled cinder blocks lay on the ground like a pile of Legos, while wisps of gray vapor threaded upward. It was the remnants of her garage.

The man picked up her coat that lay on the ground. He yelled, "Are you sure? The smoke smell is really strong, and there's ash covering most of it."

The female paramedic gazed down at her. "What did you need your coat for?"

"Box. Jewelry box inside—inside the pocket."

The EMT pointed at her partner. "Look in the pockets for a jewelry box."

He pulled the container out, dropped the coat, and walked over to them. "Here you go," he said, handing it to Gabrielle.

"Ms. Vakis, is that your wedding ring?" the woman asked.

She shook her head as she opened the top. The silver ring sat secure in the crease of the soft material. He had her ring. It was payback for Jordan taking his.

Two police officers came out of her house and walked toward her.

She closed the felt box and shoved it in her pajama pocket. Her phone wasn't there. Shivering, she slid down on the cot under the blanket. Weariness filled her.

"Where's my phone?" she asked the paramedic.

The woman nodded. "It's with your jacket. I should have had Craig bring that over as well." She gestured to the other EMT. "Hey, bring the phone too."

He bent and handed it to Gabrielle.

"Thank you."

The police officers stood over her. "Excuse me, Ms. Vakis. We need to ask you a few questions," one of them said as they frowned and stared down at her.

Before Gabrielle could protest, the EMT said, "Not now, officers. We need to get her to the hospital."

The men in blue exchanged contemplative looks before the same officer spoke. "Which hospital?"

"General," the paramedic answered. She tucked the blanket around Gabrielle's body.

"We'll see you there later, Ms. Vakis," the cop said.

Gabrielle nodded. They walked toward their car.

She glanced at the back of the ambulance again, where Jordan lay on a gurney and two other emergency medical technicians tended to him.

"Is he going to be okay?"

"Don't worry. We'll take good care of him and hand him safely over to the doctors at the hospital."

One of the EMTs hopped out of the back of the vehicle, slammed the doors shut, and jogged to the front driver's side. The van rumbled to life. With lights on, the ambulance bumped down the gravel driveway.

Gabrielle reached out her hand to the vehicle rolling away with Jordan inside.

The paramedic put her equipment away, then jutted her chin toward Craig. "Time to get her into the van."

As they carried Gabrielle to the ambulance, her mind swarmed with thoughts. The brutal forest man was still out there somewhere. She'd find out where. She had a ring for him, and he had hers. She hoped he didn't hock it before she could find him.

12

———

After a CAT scan and physical checkup showing no concussion, Gabrielle refused the doctor's suggestion to stay overnight for observation. She filled out discharge papers, then texted Karensa and her family and let her boss know she wouldn't make it to work.

She approached the nurses' station and handed over the discharge papers. "Where can I find Jordan Hardy?"

The nurse took the sheets. "Are you family?"

"Yes."

The nurse looked down at a chart of names. "Jordan Hardy is in room 307 on the third floor." She pointed toward a set of elevators down the hallway.

"Thank you." Gabrielle headed in that direction.

He lay on the white-sheeted bed with its equally white blanket covering most of his body. The top of a hospital gown covered his shoulders and chest as wires snaked out from open slots in the material below his collarbone. An oxygen tube hung out of his blackened nose. Sleeping, he wore a peaceful expression on his swollen, bruised face. A bandage circled his head with two faint stains on the right temple and forehead.

Gabrielle's heart tightened as she thought about all he'd gone through.

She crept to the side of his bed and pulled up a chair. Reaching toward him, she placed her hand over his cool, rough one. He stirred from her touch, his eyelids cracking slowly open.

"Hi, there."

"Gabby," he said in a weak voice.

"Yes." She squeezed his hand.

He scanned the room through droopy lids. "Am I in the hospital?" He tried to raise himself and winced.

She leaned over and patted his shoulder, directing him back against the pillows. "Yes, and you need to rest."

He let out a tired sigh and closed his eyes. A minute later, he fell asleep again.

The door swung open, and a doctor with a computer tablet in his hands, followed by a nurse, entered the room.

The doctor shook hands with Gabrielle. "Hello. I'm Dr. Norris."

"Gabrielle."

"Are you Jordan's wife?"

"Oh no. I'm his cousin's wife," she explained, releasing his hand. She glanced at Jordan, then at the doctor. "How is he?"

"Ah." His eyes studied the tablet. "He's suffered a couple of bruised ribs, black eyes, concussion, and a broken nose. But he'll recover in the coming weeks."

She grimaced, then sighed in relief. "Thank God he'll be okay. When can he be released?"

"In three to four days. We'll see how he's doing by the third day and determine then if he needs to stay longer."

With this information, she should have enough time to search for and find the forest man before he hocked her ring. If she got to him before the police, she could give him the ring, and hopefully he'd give her ring back, and then he'd finally leave Jordan alone.

Dr. Morris nodded with a tight smile and, along with the nurse, left the room.

"Did you hear that, Jordan?" She patted his arm. "You'll be out of here in a few days. Just rest."

GABRIELLE WAS STANDING near the ER's nurses' station when Karensa burst through the hospital doors, rushed over, and embraced her. "Thank God you're all right!" Tears swam in her ebony eyes.

She patted Karensa's back. Her friend fidgeted and gnawed on her lip, as if she were the one who had just gone through a trauma. But Gabrielle's thoughts had already shifted from the past few hours, focused on her next move.

The two police officers who were at her house earlier strode to the counter. "Ms. Vakis, good to see you're doing better," the one with the name tag DOWNS said. "Do you have a moment for some questions?"

She tensed, but she had to do this. "Yes."

"Good." Downs pointed to a hallway. "The second door on the left is a small meeting room used for family members."

"I'll be right back," she told Karensa.

"I'll be here waiting, love," she said.

The officers and Gabby entered the room. Downs's partner closed the door. They took the two chairs, and she sat on the sofa, resting her clasped hands in her lap. Downs's partner's name tag read BOWEN. He had a clipboard and paper. He pulled out a pen from his shirt pocket.

"We'll be asking you questions about this morning's attack. Please do your best to answer as accurately as possible,"

Downs said, his balding head tilted and his gray-blue eyes kind.

She nodded as she calmed her nerves. She wanted to be as honest as she could. Honest and accurate. But she also wanted to find the vagabond before they did. Despite what he'd done to Jordan and her, she needed to make things right on behalf of both of them.

"Please start at the beginning," Downs said.

Bowen stared at her with pen in hand.

Gabby relayed the story, grimacing through the memory of the bloodstained scenes and blinking back tears as she described Jordan's beaten body.

"So, you didn't see the person who attacked you?" Downs asked.

"No."

"Is Mr. Hardy a friend of yours?"

"Yes. He's my late husband's cousin."

"Does he stay at your house often?"

She shifted in her seat. "No, not really."

"Why did he spend the night at your house this time?" Downs looked at her with brows lowered in concentration.

She wrung her hands but stopped when Downs's eyes traveled to them. "He was resting... recuperating."

"From what?"

She wiped her sweaty palms on her pants. "He'd been beaten the day before."

Bowen scribbled on his paper, and Downs leaned forward. "Beaten by whom?"

She avoided his stare and shrugged. "He says it was by a homeless man at one of the shelters he goes to."

She lowered her gaze as Downs said, "You don't know who this homeless man is?"

"No."

"Or why he'd beaten up Mr. Hardy?"

Before she could answer, Bowen said, "Mr. Hardy would have the answer to that."

Downs sat back, straight in his chair. "Yes, and we'll question him soon." His eyes flicked to hers. "Would you please answer the question, Ms. Vakis?"

"Yes, of course." She smiled weakly and wove her hands together again. What would happen to Jordan if she told them he'd stolen the homeless man's ring? Would he be jailed? She licked her dry lips. She had no choice but to be honest. She'd start at the beginning of their pilfering feud.

She leaned forward. "I think the homeless man is in pain and lashing out."

"Arson is certainly a violent way of lashing out," Downs said.

"He must not be thinking straight."

"You sure know a lot about a man you said you didn't know."

She swallowed, lowering her gaze. "I'm going off what Jordan had told me about their run-ins."

"It's nothing for you to be concerned about. The crime is in our hands now," Downs said and nodded toward Bowen.

Bowen handed her his pen to sign the form.

She signed the paper as Downs's words ate at her. The situation was out of her hands. But she couldn't let it be. Their rings still needed to be exchanged and some type of peaceful resolution made.

"Thank you, Ms. Vakis. We'll be in touch," Downs said, opening the door.

Gabrielle stepped out of the room, rolling her shoulders. *Glad that's over. Now onto my mission.*

As the policemen walked out the hospital lobby doors, her mother and sister scurried in. Karensa joined her at the front counter.

"Gabrielle," her mother said, with tears in her eyes and

tissue in her hand. "I'm so grateful you're all right." She hugged her as if she was afraid to let her go.

Angie folded Gabrielle in her arms. "I'm glad you're okay." She studied her face. "This has something to do with Jordan, doesn't it?"

She didn't have time to explain, and she didn't really want to share the details with them. They'd only worry more. More importantly, with the information the police extracted from her, they'd track the homeless guy down soon enough, but she hoped not before she had the chance to track him down herself.

"Angela, honey, we can discuss Jordan later. She needs rest," Marcia said.

Thank you, Mom. Gabrielle nodded. "Yes, and Karensa's been here for the past half hour or so waiting to drive me home."

Marcia and Angie stared wide-eyed.

"But we'd like to look after you when you get home," Marcia said.

"I'll only be sleeping." She hated to lie, but it couldn't be helped.

"That's good, and we can clean up and make you something to eat when you get up." Marcia smiled.

"There may be police around my property or even in my house when I get home. It may be a while before I can nap." She looked away, uncertain any of what she'd said was true.

"What are they looking for in your house?" Angie folded her arms. "This sounds even more serious than I thought."

Marcia's mouth fell open, and her palms covered her cheeks. "Lord, what happened?"

Gabrielle's heart twisted. She reached for her mother.

Karensa patted Marcia's back. "It's okay, Mrs. Soulis. I'll make sure to have Gabby call you when she wakes from her nap." She linked her arm through Gabrielle's. "I'm taking her home now."

Gabrielle blew out a breath. *Thank you, Rensa!*

Marcia frowned, giving Gabrielle another hug. "I'll be waiting to hear from you."

KARENSA AND GABRIELLE pulled into the driveway and couldn't help but stare at the charred remains of her garage before rolling to a stop between it and the house. Yellow police tape still surrounded the garage area.

"Gabby, there's nothing left of it. Are you sure you're all right?"

"I'm fine." She ignored the slight soreness on the back of her head.

They exited Karensa's SUV, then approached the house.

A black van next to her home roared to life, then rumbled past them down the driveway.

"Oh my god. Just like on TV." Karensa gaped. "They must have dusted for fingerprints and gathered clues." She moved more slowly next to Gabrielle, as if contemplating the situation. Then she stopped abruptly and looked at Gabrielle in horror. "What happened inside your house?"

Gabrielle glanced at the van turning onto the main road. The paramedics, police cars, police questioning, and now this crime scene van made it all very real, and a chill slid down her spine. Hopefully, she wouldn't see any of them again.

"Gabby." Karensa's urgent tone broke through her thoughts.

"Nothing, really. Just some fighting." She stepped to the back door.

Karensa sidled next to her, staring at the door as if she'd expected to see a dead body behind it. Her friend had never handled graphic violence well.

"You know, I'm fine. You can go home. I'm going to sleep."

Karensa looked from the door to Gabrielle. "Sleep? Okay,

sure." She touched Gabrielle's shoulder, then stepped back from her. "Call me when you're up for company."

Karensa scampered to her car, got in, and drove off at a clipped pace.

Gabrielle stood alone in the cold morning's silence.

The rays of the yellow sun spread across the stone house and brown yard. The ghost of the garage and the forest losing the last of its leaves glared at her.

Would the homeless man still be around there when so many police had traipsed through her property? What if he fled the state with her ring? She swept the negative thought from her mind. Maybe he was injured from brawling with Jordan. Yes. She'd focus on that scenario as she planned her next move.

13

Having learned nothing about the forest man from the Lancaster shelter residents, Gabrielle parked her car by the curb in front of the homeless shelter in Columbia. Jordan had run into him at this building a month ago. Somebody had to know him there.

With the scripted words she'd use running through her mind, she entered the front doors, and warmth fanned her face. To Gabrielle's right, a brown-haired woman with a friendly, dimpled face stood behind a counter.

"Hello. Can I help you?"

Murmuring voices and clattering of dishes came from the large doorway down the hall. She glanced at it, then turned her attention to the woman. "I'm here for the soup kitchen... to eat."

"Certainly." She smiled and pointed toward the long hallway. "The first large room on the left."

"Thank you." It was nearly noon. The place should be packed with its usual visitors—ones who probably had eaten with the forest man, at least a few times.

Gabrielle walked into the cavernous room filled with tables, chairs, and a long buffet table. Various meaty and soupy aromas wafted in the air. Smiling volunteers were serving hefty portions of food on the plates of the many people lined up in front of them.

She'd guessed at least a hundred people congregated in the huge, white-walled room. A poster tacked on the wall to her left displayed the soup kitchen hours. Above the poster hung a large round clock. The three remaining walls were decorated with colorful paintings with short, uplifting quotes written within the scenes, and a plain silver cross hung over the entryway. Adult men made up most of the homeless crowd, but there were a few dozen women and families. None of the men wore a blue bandanna.

Not knowing where to start, Gabrielle tapped the first shoulder she came upon at the closest table. "Excuse me."

A man wearing a black winter hat, several layers of shirts, and a menacing frown looked up at her. "Yeah?"

She smiled. "Hello. I'm Gabby." She stuck out her hand.

He flicked a stare at it, grunted, and went back to eating mashed potatoes.

"I have a friend that comes here at times."

"So?"

"He has a friend that comes here too."

He jerked a shrug and held up his filthy palms.

"I'm trying to get in touch with his friend. I need to give him something."

He didn't respond this time.

She gingerly sat on the small foot of space on the long metal bench between him and the man next to him.

He leaned away from her, lifted his right arm in a hooked motion, and gave her an annoyed sideways glance.

"He's about six feet tall, wears a gray jacket, black boots, and jeans."

The man kept his eyes on his plate. "Don't know him."

"And he wears a blue bandanna around his head."

"Nope. Never seen him." He shoveled meat that looked like turkey into his mouth.

A bald man with a birthmark on his left cheekbone sat across from the man next to her. He jutted his stubbled chin toward her. "Rocky knows him."

The man on her right nodded, his long dreadlocks cascading down his back. "Sure does."

"So, you two have seen my friend?"

The man with the dreadlocks nodded again. "Seen him around here but not a lot in the past two or three weeks. Never talked to him though. Rocky has."

"Yeah. Like I said. Rocky and him are pretty tight," the bald-headed man added.

"How can I get in touch with Rocky? Is he here now?" she asked.

"He comes here every afternoon. Around one, one thirty," the bald-headed man said.

Gabrielle glanced at the wall clock. Twelve fifteen. "Can you tell me what he looks like so I can find him when he arrives?"

The man with the dreadlocks dropped a chunk of a dinner roll onto his tray. He wiped his mouth with a napkin and looked at her with close-set brown eyes. "He's real easy to spot. Always wears the same thing—"

"Tan pants, an old Pirates baseball cap, and a black jacket," the bald-headed man interjected.

"He's got stringy blond hair. Reaches his shoulders," dreadlocks man continued.

"Is he a young man?"

"Around forty," he replied.

"Thank you so much for your help."

"No problem," he said.

The man on her left got up, picked up his tray, and walked off. The two men she'd been talking to did the same.

Gabrielle walked out of the room, planning to return later, hoping Rocky could tell her where the forest man was.

AN HOUR LATER, Gabrielle reentered the soup kitchen. New faces and bodies occupied the benches at the various tables. Fewer families were present in the afternoon flow.

She walked between tables, scanning people who fit the description given to her by the homeless men she sat with earlier. A black Pirates cap bobbed between other heads and hats two tables down from her. She made her way to the person and slid into the open spot at the end of the bench. A man with shoulder-length, wispy blond hair and a Pirates cap faced his plate, talking to a skinny man with a large nose across from him. The slacks and coat finished off the description given to her.

"No. Didn't make it to the doors in time last night. Did you?" he asked the man across from him.

The guy shook his head. "Too busy with Cal. Jo's Restaurant's dumpster had fresh throwaways."

She tapped Rocky on the shoulder. Startled, he turned his head toward her and raised his sandy-blond brows. "Well, hello, young lady." He gave her a friendly gap-toothed smile that lit up his sun-weathered face. His hazel eyes shone with kindness.

"Hi. Are you Rocky?"

"That's what they call me." He took a sip of water from a plastic cup.

She smiled back, and tension left her body. "I was told you know a friend of mine."

He wiped his mouth with a starchy brown napkin. "I do, huh?" His eyes flicked over her. "Don't mean to sound rude, but you don't look like the type of folks that hang out here. Never seen you before. Just now homeless?"

With the exception of his slovenly hair and stained pants, he didn't look homeless. She froze. What made her think such a thing? She frowned and shook her head. Anybody could be homeless, lose their job, be sick, and end up on the streets. She knew that firsthand with Jordan.

Gabrielle straightened and placed her elbow on the table. "You're right. I've not been here before. I'm not homeless. But my good friend is and has been here often, as well as his friend. I'm looking for his friend."

He nodded. "Sure. I know a lot of the locals here. What's his name?"

Ugh. Why hadn't she thought he'd ask her such an obvious question? She smiled apologetically and pushed a strand of hair behind her ear. "I don't know—"

He let out a hearty laugh. "He's a friend, but you don't know his name?"

Her cheeks warmed. "He's really a friend of my good friend, but I know what he looks like."

"Hope it's a real good description. Nobody stands out here. Kind of look the same with our baggy clothes, hairy faces." He rubbed his stubbly cheek and grinned.

His buddy laughed as he shoveled a forkful of what looked like chicken pieces into his small mouth.

She joined in their good-natured jesting. "I hadn't noticed."

Rocky took off his cap and bowed his head. "Nice of you to say." He replaced his hat.

She tapped her fingers on the table. "So, my friend's friend is probably in his forties. He wears a gray coat, black boots and jeans, and a blue bandanna."

Rocky's demeanor changed. His face lost its glow. "Your

friend is pals with Clay?" He looked at her with doubt in his hazel eyes.

She tensed and wasn't sure what to say.

He twisted his stocky frame toward her and put a gentle, hefty hand on her shoulder. "Young lady, you and your friend don't wanna mess with Clay. He's not predictable. His moods change faster than the weather." He grimaced. "Got a nasty temper."

She grasped for a response that wouldn't come.

He saved her by saying, "Lots more bearish lately." He shook his head. "He don't have a lot of friends. Your friend's probably the only one."

Gabrielle smoothed out her sweater as she worked up her reply. "Yes, my friend told me that."

"So, what you want to meet with Clay for?"

"I have something to give him. He lost it a while back, and I... I found it and need to give it back to him." She frowned at the story she'd just made up.

"Okay." He shrugged and blew out a loud breath. "Suit yourself. Don't say I didn't warn you."

"Do you know where I can find him here?"

Rocky removed his ball cap and scratched his head. "Hasn't been here the past few days."

Gabrielle leaned forward on the table. "Do you know where else he likes to hang out?"

His eyes narrowed in thought as he set his hat back on his head. "Goes to his special hideout. That's what he calls it. Says it's the only place he finds any peace." He chuckled. "And boy does he need some. Wound tighter than a screw."

Yes! Just the information she needed. She fisted her hands in her lap. "Where is his special hideout?"

He laughed again. "You think he told me? Told anybody? Hell, no."

She rubbed her temple. *So close.* "No idea, huh?"

Rocky took a bite of a roll, then studied the piece of bread. "Said it was smack dab in the middle of a bunch of trees. Said he liked the privacy." His gaze traveled to her face. "That's all he told me."

With a feeling of satisfaction, she rose from the bench. "Thank you very much."

He shrugged. "I didn't do much."

"You did." She nodded and touched his shoulder. "I wish you the best."

Rocky's chapped lips spread into a smile. "You be careful and take care, young lady."

"I will."

Gabrielle strode to the entrance. The adrenaline rush that had run through her minutes ago dissipated, and the achiness from the struggles from early in the morning permeated her body. With a sigh, she climbed in her car and drove home. After a short, restful nap, she'd search the forest behind her house.

14

———————

The doorbell chiming woke Gabrielle from her nap. She sat up and rubbed her eyes. How long had she been sleeping? The dull, leftover pain in the back of her head returned while she stuffed her woolly socked feet into her plush bear slippers.

Another ring sounded as she descended the stairs and crossed to the messy living room. The furniture, broken lamp, and vase still lay strewn across the floor. She ran a hand through her hair. She needed to clean the room but instead glanced out the window. The last gasps of sunlight crowned the hill behind her destroyed garage. Fat white flakes cartwheeled toward the ground, already blanketed with an inch of snow. She'd missed her chance. Tomorrow morning she'd scour the woods.

A key clattered in the door's lock.

"Gabby, love, me and your mom are here," Karensa said from the other side of the door.

It opened, and Karensa and her mother came inside.

Marcia held a casserole dish, handed it to Karensa, then took Gabrielle into her soft arms. "Lord, what happened to your garage?"

Gabrielle tensed. What should she tell her? "There was an accident, but nobody was hurt…" She cringed at her lies. When would she stop lying to her mother?

Marcia let her go, frowned, and looked into her eyes. "That's a mighty bad accident, dear."

Gabrielle took her mother's hand and patted it. "It's over, and I'm fine, Mom. Please don't worry."

"Ha." Marcia's gaze traveled to the ceiling with palms up.

She rubbed her mother's back. "I'm okay, Mom. Really."

Marcia smiled, stroking the side of Gabrielle's face, but the smile morphed into a gasp, and a look of horror replaced it. "Lord—" Her mother's frightened gaze moved past her toward the living room.

"Holy sh— Er, I mean, wow." Karensa stared wide-eyed.

Gabrielle bit her lip. "I know, I know. I haven't had a chance to clean yet. I fell asleep right when I lay down."

"No worries, love," Karensa said with a grimace. She passed Marcia the casserole dish and hung her coat on one of the pegs by the door. "We'll help you tidy the place."

"Thank you."

Marcia's face pinched in that familiar look of pain she'd seen too often over the years, breaking Gabrielle's heart. She should have gone to her mother's house instead of hers. It was too much for her. She reached for her mother, but she'd already moved toward the kitchen.

"I'm going to warm this up in the oven," Marcia said. She walked into the kitchen and switched on the light. "Oh dear."

The blood spots. Gabrielle scurried into the kitchen and took the pot from her mother before it could fall from her trembling hands. "I'm sorry, Mom. As I said, I haven't had a chance to clean." She set the dish on the table.

Marcia wobbled to the table and took a seat. She wrung her hands. "Dear, what happened here?" Tears welled in her eyes.

Gabrielle swallowed hard, then squatted in front of her mother. "There was a small scuffle between Jordan and a homeless man. It wasn't that bad."

Marcia inhaled deeply, then blew out a breath. She closed her eyes, then opened them, focusing on Gabrielle. "What... What happened to Jordan?"

She pushed aside the terrible memories of Jordan's beaten body in the garage and in the hospital. "He's fine." *God, another lie.* She gazed at the ceiling, her mouth firm, disgusted with herself.

Marcia nodded, accepting her lie, and her heart twisted, along with her stomach.

"All right." Her mother surveyed the dirty floor. "Just needs a mop run across it."

"Yes." Gabrielle pulled out a Swiffer mop and pre-wet cloths from the closet. "I'll do that right now."

"Let Karensa do that, dear." Her mother slid the casserole dish into the oven and shut the door. "You've gone through a lot this morning."

"Yes. Let me, love." Karensa took the mop from Gabrielle before she could protest, attached a wet cloth to the mop head, and began gliding it across the white-tiled floor. With every thrust, the brown spots faded but didn't fully disappear.

"Going to have to use some bleach," Karensa said.

Gabrielle grabbed a bottle from the cabinet under the sink and handed it to Karensa. She squirted bleach on the bloodstained areas, then ran the mop back over the faint spots. They vanished.

Gabrielle's shoulders relaxed. She set clean dishes on the table, then stared out the window. The snowflakes had increased, falling faster and heavier. "How much snow are we supposed to get? It's coming down pretty hard right now."

Karensa put the mop back in the closet. "It's a good-sized

storm coming through. The weather guy said we're supposed to get anywhere from six to eight inches. But when has he been right?" She snickered.

Marcia tapped the buttons above the oven door, then spun around. "It's enough to be dangerous." She sat down again. "You aren't planning to go into work tomorrow, are you?"

Gabrielle shrugged and sat in the chair next to her mother. "If the office is open and people are there, then yes, I'll be too."

Marcia frowned and laid a hand on Gabrielle's arm. "Don't you need another day to recuperate?"

Gabrielle shook her head. "I'm feeling fine."

Karensa took the second to last chair at the table and sat down. "She's going to work tomorrow." She raised an eyebrow at Marcia. "You know there's no way of talking her out of it."

Marcia sighed. "Yes, I know." She turned her gaze toward Gabrielle. "Promise me you won't drive if the roads get dicey."

Gabrielle patted her mother's hand. "I promise. Don't worry."

Marcia shook her head. "Lord, how many times have you told me that, and you know it does no good." She glanced toward the living room. "Especially after the horrible things that happened here." Marcia reached toward Gabrielle and took her hand. "You must have been so scared. My poor baby girl." Tears gathered in her eyes again. "Why didn't you come home instead of back here?"

Gabrielle squeezed her mother's hand. "I'm okay, Mom. Really."

Marcia returned the squeeze. "That madman is still on the loose. I'm afraid for you."

"He thinks Jordan is dead, and I didn't see him." Gabrielle winced. She shouldn't have let that slip out. How would her mother take the man thinking Jordan had died? Would she come to the conclusion that their fight was worse than what she'd relayed?

Marcia's face paled. "Dead?"

She bit her lip and hurried to say something, veering away from talk of death. "He has no reason to come back here. Besides, the police combed this area and are keeping an eye on it." But hopefully not focusing on the woods. She needed her crack at him before they did. The nagging worry of him selling her ring and her never seeing it again made her stomach churn.

Marcia nodded. "Oh, that's good. I feel better knowing the police are guarding your house."

Gabrielle let go of her mother's hand. "See? Everything is okay." Even though she wasn't certain the police were actually guarding her house. She'd only seen them patrolling the area. But she kept her thoughts to herself.

"Trust me. I'm safe here." She raised her brows at Karensa and mouthed *Back me up.*

Karensa rested an elbow on the table and gestured toward Gabrielle. "She's right, Mrs. Soulis." Even as her friend said this, Gabrielle could see the doubt in Karensa's eyes. She didn't believe her own words.

Marcia's lips trembled. "I'm not completely convinced."

The oven buzzer went off.

Saved by dinner. Gabrielle clasped her hands together. "Great. I'm starved."

Marcia shuffled to the oven. "My chicken casserole will fill you right up."

Her mother busied herself with serving the food, seeming to have let go of her worries for a while. Gabrielle breathed a sigh of relief.

AFTER DINNER, Gabrielle convinced her mother to go home before the snow accumulated further. She and Karensa picked up the mess in the living room. She laid the broken lamp on the end table and ran a loving hand over the carved bear. Somehow the long crack in the lamp felt like a growing chasm between her and Andrew. That she'd lost another part of him in this broken object they both loved.

With a heavy heart, Gabrielle withdrew her hand from the carving and touched her bare ring finger. She'd not allow this connection to be broken. She'd get it back from Clay.

15

Gabrielle pushed open the back door into a foot of snow. The weatherman had been wrong again.

In the early-morning light, she used what was left of the metal-framed, soot-smeared shovel from the garage to clean off her back porch slab. She plowed a path through the white blanket to her car sitting by the side of the house.

Checking her watch, Gabrielle grabbed her purse and trudged to her car. She unlocked the doors with her key fob and tossed her purse onto the front passenger seat. Locking the doors, she looked toward the naked trees skirted and sprinkled with snow.

With a set jaw, she traipsed through the backyard to the forest. White puffs floated from her mouth as she moved between branches, and her boots crunched down on the frozen, snowy ground. She stopped fifty yards inside the woods and scanned the area. Her heartbeat quickened. Silence cloaked her surroundings. No birds chirped. No tree branches creaked. No wind blew. No human came plodding through the maze of wooden stalks, and no shacks or makeshift homes rose ahead of her as she stomped another ten feet forward.

Gabrielle frowned and spun around, heading back to her house. She'd not give up. After all, she'd only reached a quarter of the way through the copse of trees. She knew there was a clearing on the other side of the forest that eventually led to a couple of houses belonging to her neighbors. She'd try again tomorrow.

AFTER WORK, Gabrielle entered Jordan's hospital room and found a dark-haired, lithe woman in a red sweater, sitting on a chair pulled close to the edge of the bed. She held Jordan's hand. The headboard area of Jordan's bed was elevated, and he looked at Gabrielle as she walked toward him and the woman.

"Gabby." He jutted his chin toward her. "Glad you came."

"Of course. I had to see how you were doing." She turned toward the woman. "Hello. I'm Gabby."

The woman had a sweet face with large brown eyes and pink cheeks. She smiled at Gabrielle. "I'm Erin."

Before Gabrielle could ask how she knew Jordan, he spoke up. "She *was* my girlfriend till she moved to Reading." He sported a crooked, amused smile, his chapped lips covered in balm.

Erin air-slapped Jordan. "I'd gotten a good job there. Besides, we needed some space to figure out where we were going with this whole relationship."

Gabrielle nodded. "How did you hear about Jordan?"

"The arson actually made Reading's local news." Erin's gaze left Gabrielle and returned to Jordan. "Scared the crap out of me when they mentioned you had been attacked and nearly burned to death." She squeezed his hand, then looked back at Gabrielle. "I had to come and make sure he was all right."

Jordan's bruised face brightened. "So glad you did."

"Me too." She gave him a warm smile.

Gabrielle grinned. The way they looked at each other reminded her of the way she and Andrew had gazed at each other. Nothing else existed around them. Perhaps this was Jordan and Erin's second chance at building a true, committed relationship.

"That's wonderful." She looked at Jordan. "You're in good hands, my friend."

"Don't I know it." He grinned.

Their reunion was fortuitous timing. Gabrielle glanced at them. Yes. Erin would be there for Jordan while she searched for Clay.

"Gabby, did the cops get the guy?" he asked.

She'd known he'd bring up what happened yesterday morning. She'd prepared to tell him what little she knew. But she wouldn't divulge her plan to look for Clay. "No, they didn't catch him. He was apparently gone by the time they got to my house."

"Do they have any leads?"

"I'm sure they've gotten tips on his whereabouts. Don't worry. He'll be caught soon." She forced what she hoped was a convincing smile.

"They'll get him, Jordan. Just concentrate on getting well," Erin added.

Gabrielle pointed in the direction of the door. "I've got to get going. I'll come visit you in the next few days." She gestured toward Erin. "In the meantime, you've got a kind, beautiful woman here for you."

Erin gave her an appreciative smile.

Jordan raised a hand in farewell. "See you later."

As the sun rose above the hill by her house, Gabrielle trekked back into the forest. The weather had stayed below freezing since yesterday morning. She followed the stamped-on path through the snow and trees and moved farther into the deep heart of the woods. The noiselessness echoed yesterday's visit. But this time the silence broke to the left of where she stood. Her gaze flicked in that direction. Someone had built a fort out of tree branches and a ratty old blanket. The plaid cover was spread over the mound of long pieces of wood.

Gabrielle stepped toward the hut twenty feet from her. Just as her boots mashed down the foot of snow a few feet away, the blanket flipped up and Clay appeared, still wearing his blue bandanna. Her heart nearly stopped as she caught her breath.

Clay's dirty gray complexion paled. But a second later, redness blotted his face as he marched toward her, kicking up clumps of snow in his path.

She stood stiffly and gripped the felt box in her pocket.

His beady eyes locked on her as he got closer. "You stupid or something? Showing your face?"

She swallowed hard, disdain and fear lodged in her throat. "I could ask you the same thing."

"You don't got the strength to bring me in. Got nobody with you either. Real stupid."

He lunged forward, his chest and face now inches from hers. His heavy breathing punctured the dead quiet of the snow-packed forest.

She closed her eyes. *Don't let him see your fear.*

Callused, cold hands wrapped around her throat. She opened her eyes in terror, looking into the wild eyes of an enraged man.

"You were Jordan's nursemaid."

She blinked, paralyzed. Icy chills ran through her.

"Your nursing wasn't enough." His grip tightened.

She gasped. *The ring! The ring!* Frantically pulling the box out of her pocket, she raised her hand. "Your... ring—"

She coughed and grabbed one of his arms with her other hand, trying to yank it off her throat. His arm didn't budge.

His stare flicked to the box in her swaying hand. "What ring?"

"Your ring."

"My ring." He eyed her with skepticism.

"Yes. Your ring... and mine."

"Jordan told you he stole my wife's ring?" He raised his chin and glowered at her.

"Your wife's ring?"

Clay studied her, as if contemplating whether what she said was the truth. She kept her eyes on his and swallowed with effort against his hands.

He took one of his hands from her neck and pointed at her. "You and him never known that." He scowled. Then a creepy smile slid across his face, revealing brown-stained teeth. "Oops. You never known. Jordan's..." He ran a finger across his throat. He wheezed a gravelly laugh.

Just as she'd expected, he thought Jordan had died. This would be to her advantage.

Gabrielle shook loose from his one-handed grip and took a step back. "You're right. We didn't know." With shaky hands, she opened the jewelry box and showed him.

He eyed it with a stony frown. "It ain't my wife's."

"I'm sorry. It's gone."

The man's face flushed. He grabbed her again, one hand on her throat, the other twisting her arm against her back and pressing her body against his. He glared and huffed out a white cloud smelling of stale cigarettes.

She ignored the ache in her arm and her queasy stomach. *This is for Jordan and all of us.* "Take the ring. It's real silver."

"Like I said…" His eyes darted to the ring again. The shiny silver gleamed in the snowy white surrounding them.

Please take it. Her arm burned. She winced and concentrated on the ring.

He let go of her, snatched the box from her shaking hand, and pushed her away. She fell into a mound of snow. He slipped the ring on his left pinky finger. She exhaled in relief.

"It ain't the original, but it'll have to do."

Now that he had his, she wanted hers. "Please, can I have mine back?"

He snorted with eyes narrowed.

Keep talking. Keep him there. She got to her feet and brushed off the snow clinging to her legs. "You know, we have something in common."

Amusement flashed through his steely gray eyes. "Like what?"

"You lost your wife, and I lost my husband."

"Jordan?" He lifted his gnarly, hairy chin.

"No, Andrew. Six months ago, almost seven now." *If only you were here with me now, Andrew.* Her heart ached for him.

His features softened. "Delores's been gone four months." He sniffed and wiped his bulbous nose.

"I'm sorry… What is your name?" she asked, even though she knew it.

He looked at her with a flushed expression of suspicion.

"You know Jordan's name." She put a palm to her chest. "I'm Gabby. It's only fair."

"Joe Smith." He snickered.

No matter. She'd play along. "I'm sorry, Joe."

He bobbed his head, planted his hands on his bulky hips, and stared at the ground. "Married fifteen years."

She gaped. "That's a long time."

He didn't respond.

"Andrew and I were married eight years."

He scoffed and gave her a sideways glance. "Friggin' babes."

His cynical words cut her. Her hands fisted as heat rose in her. "We didn't get the chance at fifteen years." She staved off the moisture collecting in her eyes.

Clay's features softened once more, and a rugged sigh came out of him. He stuffed his left hand into his ratty coat pocket. His hand came out holding her gold band.

Gabrielle didn't move, not wanting to disrupt his actions for which she'd been waiting so long. She kept her eyes on his, standing straight as a pin, and stowing away the constant fear that had been coursing through her.

With only a foot's distance between them, Clay held up his grimy hand. "Take it."

She reached slowly for the band, then slipped it on her ring finger where it had always belonged. It would stay there forever, just as Andrew would be in her heart eternally. "Thank you."

He grunted and lumbered off at a quick pace into the bare-branched thicket.

Running her left hand over her ring, she could barely believe this encounter had happened. Her plan had been a success for all of them. Jordan would be fine. No doubts filled her head.

She glanced in the direction in which Clay had gone. He'd lost his wife only four months ago. She remembered that feeling of loss four months after Andrew's shocking death. Her heart had still been broken, left gaping and raw. Clay must have been feeling something akin to that.

Gabrielle stared at the makeshift wooden hut. Where would he go now? The police would eventually catch up with him. A part of her wished they wouldn't.

16

——

Two weeks later, Gabrielle and Jordan sat on the sofa in the living room, eating meatloaf she'd made for dinner. The bruises had faded from Jordan's face, and his ribs gradually mended. He'd been staying at her home since his release from the hospital four days ago. During that time, she'd spoken with Tom, the human resource manager.

"I can't wait until tomorrow morning. My first interview in years." Jordan grinned, then took a gulp of apple cider from his cup.

She surveyed his appearance. "You will be showering and doing something with the hair on your face before the interview, right?"

"Nope. Thought I'd go in looking like Alan Parish just coming out of the *Jumanji* game board." Jordan winked.

She laughed. It was nice to see him at ease and in high spirits. Until now, she'd only seen snippets of this side of him.

Gabrielle took her plate to the kitchen sink, then headed to the kandelia to check the oil and wick. The humble flame still burned. She added just enough oil to the cup to get the cork floating and wick rising. Its glow spread against the wall and icons. The light emitted a spark of warmth. She closed her eyes and absorbed the solace the sacred space always gave her.

Andrew's anniversary gift had never left her thoughts. But she'd put it aside until the past few days when Jordan had recovered. They'd searched the house but had come up empty.

His shoes shuffled on the kitchen tile. She pivoted from the prayer shelf and trailed behind him.

"Do you need help washing these?" he asked, pointing to the sink half-full of dishes.

She waved a hand in dismissal. "Not right now. I'd like to do some snooping around for Andrew's present."

"All right." He leaned against the counter. "Where do you want to start this time?"

"The bedrooms again." She pointed a thumb behind her. "I'll take my bedroom, and you take the extra one."

"Got it."

Once on the second floor, they entered their assigned rooms. The extra bedroom had become Jordan's while staying with her.

As Gabrielle heard things being moved about from his room, she opened the closet door and grabbed the safe box on the floor by Andrew's shoes. She hadn't bothered to look there before now. It was an obvious place to stash money and other valuables. Still, Andrew might have stored the money in there anyway.

She strode to her jewelry box on the small table in the corner of the room and plucked the key from one of its drawers. Turning the key and lifting the heavy gray lid, she dug in the box for anything unfamiliar. But nothing emerged from beneath their wedding license, social security cards, or birth certificates.

She locked it, put the key in the jewelry drawer, and sighed. It had been worth the try.

Setting the safe box on the closet floor, she spotted the three shoeboxes on the top shelf above the hanging clothes. The first box on the left she knew contained sewing materials, and the blue box with brown wrapping tape that sat farthest to the right held Andrew's baseball cards. The yellow box in the middle pushed back farther than the other two stumped her. How had she missed it the last time she rummaged in the closet? Her curiosity rose.

On tiptoes, she stretched up and pulled the box down. It had some weight to it. Gabrielle laid it on the bed and removed the lid. Recognition hit her when she saw the thin stack of documents neatly placed in the container.

Her lips quivered as she lifted the pages out and skimmed over the typed, professional forms with their names and personal information written in blue ink. The adoption papers they'd never finished. It had taken so much out of them. The endless red tape, legal hurdles. But worst of all, the searing heartache they'd experienced finding themselves without sufficient savings to finish the process. The past pain of their struggles for a child stabbed her heart. They'd had so many plans. They'd barely begun their love story when the tragic crash took Andrew away from her.

Don't travel to the past. Accept the present. You've been doing so well lately.

Gabrielle set the papers neatly in the box, replaced the lid, and pushed it back on the closet shelf.

No other unknown boxes were in there, so she slid the doors closed and looked around her room for any other places to store things.

Footsteps creaked on the wooden floor in the hallway. Jordan appeared at her bedroom door. "Nothing in that room."

With one last scan of the area, she moved toward him. "Nothing here either."

THE PINK of morning poured through the kitchen windows, casting a rosy tint over the beige counters and white-tiled floor. The dangling light fixture over the table shed a flush of yellow onto it.

As Gabrielle walked to the pantry to pull out a box of cereal, shoes clacked on the hardwood floor in the living room. She pivoted toward the doorframe to the kitchen, and her mouth fell open. Jordan stood in the entryway to the kitchen. At least she believed the man wearing her husband's suit was Jordan. It was hard to tell without the scraggly facial hair, unkempt mane, or bedraggled clothes.

He stood tall, beaming, his eyes sparkling. His face was scrubbed clean, his chin, cheeks, and around his mouth, smooth and hairless. Jordan's dishwater-blond, wavy hair was brushed back, neatly tucked behind his ears. Andrew's suit fit perfectly, and the navy color brought out Jordan's remarkable eyes.

As Jordan posed there, his image faded, replaced by Andrew's. He smiled, the kind of smile that lit up his whole face and everything around him. Gabrielle grinned. But a second later, he was gone, and Jordan's figure returned.

Jordan lifted his arms to the side. "I look okay then?"

"You do."

"It's amazing what soap and a razor can do." He chuckled and moved to the pantry.

She sniggered and set hot mugs on the table. "Tea's ready."

"Great. Thanks." He put a box of Cheerios on the table, then located the milk in the fridge.

She retrieved the bowls and spoons. She kept glancing his way, still amazed by the transformation.

"You're staring again," he said and ran a hand over his head. "Do I really look *that* different?"

"I almost didn't recognize you," she blurted out.

His eyes widened.

"I just mean that... Well, what do you expect? I couldn't see what was under that unkempt beard." She gave him a sheepish smile, then raised her brows. "I wonder if Erin will recognize you."

"She will, and she'll be doing backflips when she sees the beard's gone." He laughed.

"So, you two are on the road to reunion?"

Jordan smoothed down his shirt and grinned. "Already have."

She put a hand on his shoulder. "I'm so happy for you."

"Yeah. She's willing to make us a top priority, and that scores big in my book since she's willing to be with a bum."

She chuckled. "You're not a bum."

"Yeah, I'm thinking not for much longer."

"That's the spirit."

He looked down at his clothes. "Do I look decent for this interview? I want to look as professional as possible."

"Yes. Andrew's suit fits you well." She poured milk into her cereal bowl.

"I noticed that when I put it on. Really fits just right." He tugged on the lapels of his suit jacket, then reached for the milk carton.

"What time is your interview? Did you say ten?"

"No, eleven thirty. By the time I'm finished, it'll be lunchtime, which works perfectly with your schedule. You can drive me back here so I don't have to hang around the office, looking out of place."

"You're right. That's good timing. I can drive us back home, eat lunch, and go back to work after that." She glanced at the suit again. "What are you planning to change into after we get back home?"

His brows knitted. "I don't know." He gestured toward the living room. "I guess back into my old clothes."

The bedroom closet and bureau full of Andrew's clothes came to her mind. "You can have some of Andrew's clothes."

His face turned pink, and his eyes shone with gratitude. "Gabby, I don't know what to say."

"Say yes. Andrew would have offered them to you if he were here." She took a bite of cereal.

Jordan left his chair and embraced her. He'd become like a brother to her. Much like he had been to Andrew.

"Thanks so much."

"You're welcome."

"I hope I get this job."

She held up her fist. "I'm rooting for you."

"And Gabby," Jordan said in a determined tone. "We'll look again for Andrew's stash tonight when you're home from work."

Rising from her chair, she gave him a thumbs-up.

He clacked across the tiles to the living room. "I'll have to go without my coat. It's too dirty and worn out to wear."

"Didn't I just say you could have some of Andrew's clothes?"

"Yeah, but this is a short trip."

"You're sure you'll be warm enough?" she asked, entering the den to grab her coat and purse.

"I'll survive."

She nodded with an assured smile. "Yes, you will."

17

When Gabrielle returned home and walked to the back door, Jordan appeared at its window with a huge grin. He yanked the door open with gusto.

"I got the job!" he shouted with his arms out to his sides.

She squealed and embraced him. "This is fabulous news. Congratulations!"

She kissed his cheek, then entered the kitchen, closing the door behind her. "When do you start?"

"Next week." He padded into the living room, wearing Andrew's socks.

"That's great." She hung her coat and set her purse on the end table by the bear lamp. She'd last seen it lying cracked on its side. It no longer lay in ruin.

She gasped. "Jordan! Did you fix this for me?"

"Yep." He sat on the couch and swung his legs onto the coffee table.

She stepped over to him. "Thank you so much. You know how much that lamp means to me."

"I do. Andrew told me you fell in love with it when you were vacationing in Estes Park." His eyes twinkled.

Jordan's whole demeanor had changed since she'd encountered him in the parking lot by the dumpster several weeks ago. Happiness painted his face. Confidence shown in his lifted chin, smile, and relaxed position on the couch. Yes. His life had completely transformed from hopelessness to promise by the new job at her company and his and Erin's reunion.

He glanced at her. "I'm going to be working at their new Allentown office that opened six months ago. So, I'll be looking for a place starting tonight, if you'll let me use your laptop."

"Of course."

"And..." He gestured to a pot on the stove. "I made us some excellent mac and cheese for dinner."

She laughed. "You're full of surprises. Thank you."

"Yep." He scooped up the pasta into two bowls. "And the sooner we eat, the sooner we can get back to searching for Andrew's gift."

She turned to face him, and he gave her a wink. Andrew's sweet face floated in her mind as a flood of loving memories of him cradled her. "Thank you."

AFTER SEARCHING the living room and crossing into the kitchen, Gabrielle peeked out the window toward the driveway. A terrible realization hit her like a bucket of ice water to the face. She hugged herself to take away the chill.

"Where's a good place to start in here?" Jordan's voice floated over her shoulder.

She swung around. "Jordan."

He glanced at her while opening the pantry door.

"What if Andrew hid our anniversary gift in the garage?"

His hand dropped off the knob.

She massaged her temple, not wanting to face this possibility.

"If he hid it there, it's toast, obviously." Jordan's tone was matter-of-fact, but his eyes showed empathy.

"What are the odds...?"

"Not very good."

"Not very good? Meaning?"

"I don't see him leaving a bunch of money in the garage. It's not a safe place for valuables."

She looked through the window at the orange glimmer on the horizon. "You're right. That wouldn't make sense."

"So, on to looking around in here." Jordan rummaged in the pantry, moving cans and boxes of food around.

Gabrielle took a deep breath and bent down to open base cabinets full of pots and pans, taking them out to look behind and inside ones in the back that she'd not used in the past year. Nothing.

After scouring the kitchen, they tried the bathrooms, even though the likelihood of finding the gift in them was extremely low. She went back upstairs and searched the extra bedroom herself, coming up empty. When she came back downstairs, Jordan was searching the bookcase in the living room again. This time he opened every book, as if expecting something to fall out of their pages. Nothing tumbled out.

They flopped onto the couch.

"Where next?" he asked.

"There are no other rooms." She frowned. "What else can we do?" Her heart sank. She was about to do something she swore she'd never do—give up.

Jordan put his arm around her shoulders. "Think, Gabby. You know Andrew better than anybody. What would be a perfect, safe spot to keep your anniversary gift?"

Sighing, she scanned the den for the fourth time. Where had

she missed? What spot was important to both her and Andrew that would have been the best place to hide their money for their trip?

The yellow glow of the humble flame in the oil lamp flickered, catching her attention. The icon shelf? She left the couch and stepped toward it, as if it were drawing her there. But she'd already looked there, hadn't she? Maybe the table? Its tiny drawer? She gently pulled it open. Two prayer bracelets and a lighter lay in it.

"Nothing in here," she said.

He came alongside her and stared at the icon shelf, then the icons themselves.

The icons.

Her eyes traveled over Christ, Saint Andrew, and archangel Gabriel. Their halos glowed golden, and they gazed serenely back at her. Inexplicable warmth filled her, and peace lit her soul as her eyes landed on her patron Saint Gabriel, the archangel—the protector, the messenger. Raising her hand to the eleven-by-fourteen-inch wooden painting, she removed it from the wall. A six-inch tall ceramic grizzly bear knickknack sat in the alcove in the wall. Gabrielle had forgotten about the alcoves since she and Andrew had moved into the house five years ago. The wall had two of them that had been there to set knickknacks, but instead they'd put up their icons and shelf.

The grizzly was sitting by a stream with a salmon in its mouth. Gabrielle grinned. *Of course.* She should have known he'd add to their bear collection, which made it a perfect gift for both of them. She blinked back tears as an ocean of emotions washed over her. Gabrielle reached for the bear. Something clattered inside it. She raised her brows and looked at Jordan.

He shrugged. "He must have stashed the money inside the figurine."

She set the ceramic figure on the coffee table and sat on the couch. Jordan joined her. She turned and tilted the painted grizzly this way and that, looking for an opening.

"Try the head," Jordan said, pointing at the top of the figurine.

She grasped the hard head and pulled gently, but it didn't move.

"The middle?" he suggested.

She gripped her hand over the top half of the bear and pulled. Nothing.

"Twist it." He gestured with his hands.

She began to turn the top section of the figurine. It moved, and the top separated from the bottom. She removed it, and a piece of paper wrapped around a roll of money peeked halfway out of the bottom of the bear.

Gabrielle gasped. "There's the money."

"Yep." Jordan rested his elbows on his knees and laced his fingers together. "His saved stash for your honeymoon."

She couldn't speak. He'd saved this money for their trip to Belize. Gabrielle shook her head in disbelief, then plucked out the fat roll. Setting the scrolled letter to the side, she flattened the pile of bills. How much had he saved?

"Want me to count it while you read the note?" Jordan asked.

Still stunned by finding this treasure, Gabrielle only nodded and picked up the paper.

She unrolled it and read it aloud. "My dearest Gabrielle." She let out a giggle.

"Okay, I'm missing something." Jordan cocked a brow. "What's so funny?"

Tears in her eyes, Gabrielle gave him a wide smile. "That's what he'd call me when he was in one of his romantic moods. He'd said it had sounded more beautiful and poetic and more so written down."

Jordan gave a nod of approval. "He's right."

She focused her attention back on the paper.

I had to get this grizzly for our home. At the store, he'd growled at me to take him with me. And you know I couldn't refuse. He was the last part of your anniversary gift I bought, so I had a fitting place to store the money I'd been saving up for the past three years.

Her voice cracked, and she wiped a tear from her cheek.

Jordan's hand squeezed her shoulder.

She nodded to let him know she was fine, then returned to Andrew's letter.

So, as you'll count out, I managed to save seven hundred dollars. It was quite a challenge. And after two years of scraping, I got a bit desperate and wondered if I'd ever get enough saved up for our well-deserved honeymoon. So, I took on another strategy, even though it wasn't much of a winning one, but when you're desperate, you try anything.

Gabrielle scrunched her face. *A new strategy? Desperate? Try anything?* Those words didn't give her warm fuzzies.

Jordan set down the stack of money and shrugged.

She continued. "That key." She sat up, startled. "Wait. What key?"

Jordan jutted his chin toward the figurine. "Must be inside there."

She leaned over and peeked inside the bear. There was a small, silver key sitting on the bottom of the knickknack. She turned over the lower section of the grizzly, put out her other hand, and the key tumbled into her palm. Turning the item back and forth with her fingers, she examined it, then set it on the table. She picked up the letter again.

Sweetie, it fits in the lock of a safe-deposit box at our bank. I opened it two months ago and put your gift in it. The number is 549. Go get your present, and I'll be waiting at home for you. Oh, and I must warn you. I don't think I'll be able to top this anniversary gift.

She set down the letter and rested her elbows on her knees and heel of her hands on her forehead.

"Wow. Didn't expect that," she heard Jordan say.

She gave him a sideways glance, still leaning on her hands. "I had no idea he did all this. The sneak." She laughed before her shoulders shook and tears poured from her eyes.

Jordan leaned into her and put an arm around her. "A sneaky but amazing guy."

Gabrielle nodded and sopped up her face with the sleeve of her shirt.

"You going to go tomorrow to the bank and see what he left you?"

"Yes. I'll go on my lunch break." She took his hand in hers. "Come with me."

Jordan grinned. "I wouldn't miss it."

18

———

Inside the bank the following morning, Gabrielle passed Jordan, who was told to wait outside the safe-deposit box room. She followed the bank employee to the steel square among others, with the numbers 549 across it. The bank employee unlocked the door, swung it open, and gestured to Gabrielle for the locked box inside.

"Let me know when you're finished, and I'll lock everything back up." The woman nodded and left the room.

Gabrielle inhaled a couple of cleansing breaths, then inserted the key, turned it all the way to the left, and slowly pulled the drawer out. She carried it to the table near the wall of deposit boxes and set it on its surface.

She blew out a breath again, then lifted the metal lid. Several stacks of one-hundred-dollar bills wrapped in red ribbon tied in bows filled nearly all the rectangular space, outlining a folded piece of paper in the center. Her jaw dropped as she took in the unbelievable sight. She'd never seen so much money in her life.

"Where'd you get all that money?" she said aloud.

Gabrielle tore her gaze from the contents in the box and unfolded the paper.

My Dearest Gabrielle,

Surprise! I know, I know. It's a boatload of money, but don't worry. I didn't rob a bank. Ha ha.

She smiled. *I'm glad you didn't.* She laughed at her unspoken response.

I told you I got desperate to scrape up money to save, so I decided to play the lotto. Yeah, I know. We never play the lotto, but like I said, I was desperate. I started playing it back before last Christmas. And, well... after several months of playing weekly, I won a portion of the winnings. Two hundred and fifty thousand dollars' worth.

Gabrielle gasped and laid a hand to her chest. She stepped back on jelly legs.

She looked at the money again. *There's actually two hundred and fifty thousand dollars in there. Good God.* She pressed a palm to her forehead and blew out a breath.

She then focused on Andrew's handwriting once more.

It was hard keeping this hidden from you. I was so excited when I won but wanted it to be the best anniversary surprise ever. I'm sure it is. Wish I could have been there to see your face when you read this, but I was working, and we'll have plenty of time to gaze into each other's eyes on our trip to Belize.

Gabrielle's heart sank, and she blinked away tears.

I thought we could pay off my student loan and the rest of our mortgage. Just a little over fifty thousand left on our house. But this money means more than a few nagging bills. It not only means we're going to Belize, but it also means we can finally adopt a child! The son we've been wanting so much. It tore us apart when we couldn't scrape up the money. Now our dreams are coming true, Gabrielle. Everything is falling into place. Our honeymoon, our child, and our little stone house are ours forever.

She wiped her eyes. Their long-awaited dream of being parents. Their little stone house. Theirs forever. Her knees gave way, and she crumpled to the floor, the letter floating down next to her.

Andrew had planned all this for them, but he wouldn't be there with her when she received the deed of their home, to pack his bags as she packed hers for their long-awaited honeymoon. And there would be no adoption without him.

An aching wave of emotions surged inside her, and she covered her face, releasing sobs.

"Gabby? Gabby, are you okay?"

She heard Jordan's voice by the entryway to the room.

Gabrielle scrubbed her face with her sleeve, grabbed the letter, and pushed herself off the floor. "I— I'm okay. I'll be out soon."

She gazed at the last words in the letter.

So, first things first, we'll take a small chunk of that money with us to Belize.

Happy anniversary, sweetheart. You're everything to me.

With all my love,

Andrew

Gabrielle fumbled for her purse and rummaged through it for tissue. She blew her nose, dried her cheeks, pushed aside the what-could-have-beens, and focused on the present. She plucked a couple of stacks of hundred-dollar bills from the steel box before shutting it. Sliding the wad of cash into her purse, she then put the box in its slot and locked it.

She glanced at the ceiling. *Thank you, thank you, my love.*

The bank employee, who stood a few feet from the entryway, alongside Jordan, waved at Gabrielle with the other key to the safe-deposit box in her hand. "All done, ma'am?"

"Yes."

The woman walked to the wall of metal slots, closed the door to 549, and locked it.

Gabrielle followed the lady out of the room.

Jordan held out his arms with his brows raised. "Well?" He spread his fingers. "You can't leave me in suspense."

She shook her head and smiled. "No, I can't." She handed him the letter.

He read it, his mouth falling open. He frowned, then smiled with sympathy shining in his eyes. He gathered her in his arms, and they cried together in what she believed was both sorrow and joy. But the sorrow dissipated as the joy lingered and buoyed her spirits. She had so much to do.

Jordan laughed. "He outdid himself."

Gabrielle shook her head. "That's the understatement of the century."

Jordan tapped the letter with his index finger. "Andy's got it all covered for you."

"He always managed to."

She folded the note, slipped it in her coat pocket, then pulled out a small stack of the bills, took Jordan's hand, and placed the money in it.

Jordan shook his head. "No. You've given me enough already."

She pressed her hand over his. "Take it. Use it for a deposit on your Allentown apartment."

He passed the money from his hand into hers. "No."

"Let me do this last thing."

Jordan sighed. "I know. It's what Andrew would want you to do."

Gabrielle straightened her posture. "No. It's what *I* want to do."

Jordan tilted his head to the side and put his hands on his hips. "You are stubborn as hell."

She grinned. "I learned from the best."

She put the bills back in his hand before he embraced her again.

"Thanks, Gabby."

"You're welcome."

She locked elbows with Jordan, and they headed out of the building.

***

IN MID-JUNE, Gabrielle sat in the passenger seat of Karensa's car as she was driven to the airport. Jordan rode with them in the back seat.

They arrived and walked down the open area toward the check-in desk.

Gabrielle rolled her suitcase toward the security checkpoint. Turning, she hugged Jordan, then Karensa.

"Have a great time, love," Karensa said.

"Take it easy and have fun." Jordan held up a thumb and grinned.

Gabrielle waved at them, then headed for her gate.

Soon she found her window seat on the plane and gazed at the blue sky. A familiar, cozy warmth embraced her. Joy lifted her heart. Andrew was with her and had always been.

Gabrielle settled in for her and Andrew's journey to Belize.

THE END

ABOUT THE AUTHOR

Dorothy Robey's debut novel, *Passage of Promise*, was published on May 1, 2020. Her second novel, *What She Didn't Know*, was published March 1, 2021. Dorothy also wrote *The Rocky Retreat* under her pen name Dorothea Anna. She lives with her family in beautiful Colorado.

facebook.com/dorothy.robey.7

twitter.com/Dotwriter3